THE BARON GOES

The door was wide open.

Before Mannering could reach them, Griselda pushed the man into the narrow passage, and he staggered helplessly. The flurry and rustle of the woman's movements made a sound like the wings of a hundred birds. The man began to protest in a weak and whining voice but the girl uttered no sound at all.

Mannering followed them, recognising the acute danger. Griselda had gone berserk, was beating and pushing the old man blindly, and he was only a few feet from the head of the stairs. If he fell, he would break his neck. But it would be useless to call out.

Mannering stepped behind Griselda, but she took no notice of his hands at her shoulders. He could feel the wiry strength of her body, muscles so taut that they seemed like sinews. The old man's eyes were closed and he was whimpering. There was a scratch, vivid red, beneath his right eye.

Mannering thrust his arms round Griselda's waist, and wrenched her away. She was so surprised that she didn't resist. He put in so much effort that, still holding her, he staggered back, her weight against him. For a moment of alarm he thought he would go crashing down on his back.

By exerting all his strength, he saved himself.

He did not save the old man, who turned round blindly and began to run, oblivious of the stairs, and as Mannering shouted: "Careful! Careful!" he went over the stairs, treading on air.

And then he crashed down.

**Also by the same author,
and available in Coronet Books:**

Nest Egg for the Baron
The Baron Goes Fast
Black for the Baron
Sport for the Baron
The Baron and the Arrogant Artist
Help from the Baron

The Baron goes a-buying

John Creasey
as Anthony Morton

CORONET BOOKS
Hodder and Stoughton

Copyright © 1971 John Creasey

First published in Great Britain by
Hodder and Stoughton 1971

Coronet edition 1975

Printed and bound in Great Britain for
Coronet Books, Hodder and Stoughton,
St. Paul's House, Warwick Lane,
London, EC4P 4AH
By Richard Clay (The Chaucer Press), Ltd.,
Bungay, Suffolk

ISBN 0 340 19865 6

CONTENTS

1

GREAT DAY

"Today," remarked John Mannering to his wife, "is the great day."

Lorna Mannering, still half-asleep, looked at him from her misty grey eyes, and asked:

"What is so great about it?"

"Well," replied Mannering, his tone and his expression changing with his mood, "any morning when you look as lovely as you do this morning has the promise of a great day."

He leaned over her and kissed her lightly on the forehead. As his lips touched her she put her arm round him, slowly, and held him. She wore a flimsy nightdress, for the weather was warm. Her shoulders and arms were like alabaster, but as soft as a child's. There was a trick of reflected light; sunlight; a shaft came in at the wide-open window and caught an old Jacobean mirror, faintly spotted and yellowed with age, and was turned on to Lorna's face and shoulders, making them glow.

Mannering drew back, a little breathless. The room was long and narrow, half-panelled, with dark furniture of several periods along the walls, a tall Victorian mirror, a rich bottle-green carpet. The bed had a magnificently-carved head panel, being made from an old Italian fireplace; and a foot panel as rare as a fifteenth-century reredos.

"Darling," he said, "don't tempt me. I must be at the shop by nine-fifteen. I really must."

"John," she said. "You are the most handsome man I've ever known."

"And *you* are the most beautiful woman *I* have ever known, and after being married for nearly thirty years I want nothing more than to stay here with you, but—"

She pulled him a little lower, a glint in her now clear—not misted—eyes.

"You must be at the shop by nine-fifteen this morning. You really must. Oh, what it is to be married to a shop-keeper!" She drew his face down and kissed him lightly on the lips. "But for one thing, I wouldn't let you go."

"What's the one thing?"

"I've remembered why you must," she answered. "It's Bill Bristow's first day. He's due at Quinns at half-past nine and you want to make sure everything is right when he arrives."

"Should I?" demanded Mannering.

"I think you're the kindest and most human man I've ever known, too," declared Lorna. "Yes, of course you should." Her eyes gleamed, near-wickedly. "No matter what the sacrifice!"

.   .   .   .

About four miles away from the Mannerings' flat in Chelsea, ex-Chief Superintendent William Bristow, until a month ago the senior detective at New Scotland Yard, stood naked to the waist at the open window of his bedroom and looked through a gap in the blocks of apartments set high on Putney Hill in the south-west of London. The room was square and plain, the furniture contemporary twenty-five years ago. Acquired as much by his wife as by himself, it had no distinction but good taste. Bristow saw the grass and the trees of Putney Heath and, far beyond, the trees of Wimbledon Common heavy with leaf.

He breathed deeply; not truly exercising, but from force

of habit. He liked to begin his days this way; it was a bridge between the night's stillness and the day's bustle.

And this day above all days must be started properly.

He smiled, but there was a hint of tension in his expression, as his mind carried him back over the years that he had known John Mannering. Why, Mannering had become part of his life!

Bristow was not a big man, and most people would have regarded him in his well-cut suit as of medium build, but here his considerable depth of chest and thickness of shoulder showed; and the flatness of his stomach, rare in a man of approaching sixty. There wasn't an ounce of superfluous flesh on him. And he had returned only a day or two ago from a holiday in Malta, with his wife Ethel, and so he was as brown as the proverbial berry. He looked as fit as a man could be. His tanned face threw grey eyes into relief so that they looked almost silver; and as he stood there, the slight tension eased until his face as well as his body was completely relaxed.

He heard his wife call: "Bill, Bill dear. Breakfast!"

He called back as he turned, and opened the door of his wardrobe. There were seven suits in the main section, two summer-weight ones in the other, and he stood back and considered. Beneath the suits were seven pairs of shoes. Just as each suit was immaculate, so was each pair of shoes; none showed any sign of wear. He picked out a pale grey summer-weight, hesitated, glanced out at the blue sky and its promise of July warmth, put the suit back and brought out one of the standard weights, darker than the other.

He dressed with great care, and was knotting a gold-coloured tie when his wife called again.

"Bill! You don't want to be late this morning of all mornings!"

"Coming!" he called.

He felt exasperated by her, and guilty because of it. Theirs hadn't been an exciting married life and he had always regarded his wife as having no imagination and little feeling, but at a time of crisis a few months before, she had been remarkably loyal and understanding. He should not feel impatient, but he did. Nevertheless when he reached the kitchen with its long window overlooking the courtyard and the traffic of Putney Hill, his expression was urbane enough. In fact, the sight of bacon crisply grilled and eggs perfectly fried, golden-looking toast and piping hot coffee, touched him with guilt again.

"Is it all right, dear?" Ethel asked.

"Lovely," he answered tritely.

"Are you ready for more toast?"

"No. This will do fine."

"I do hope the coffee's right."

"Perfect," he assured her.

She fussed until, at a few minutes to nine, he was ready to leave. It was natural that he should be eager, natural that he should be impatient, but she was just that little bit too insistent. She stood, now, in front of him, one hand behind her, and put her face up to be kissed.

He kissed her cheek.

"I hope you have a wonderful first day," she said, and drew her hand from behind her back. In it was a white gardenia, quite fresh, with curiously fragile-looking perfection; almost like a snowflake.

She pushed the short stem through his buttonhole, and pinned it the other side, while he stood rigidly at attention. In all the mornings he had left his home for the Yard, she had never done this he had always bought a gardenia from an old woman at a flower stall at Putney Station, and the flower seller had pinned it on. Why on earth had his wife chosen this morning—

"There, dear, it looks beautiful."

"Just right," he said, gruffly. "Thanks. Must go."

She opened the door for him, and he went out spruce and brisk, to the lift, the courtyard, and Putney Hill. Ruffled, mostly with himself, he stood at the entrance to the apartments complex, and looked up the hill. The sun shone warm, the traffic was noisy and fast, mostly going downhill towards the bridge, the West End and the City. But he continued to look uphill, towards another, much more modern apartment building. This was built on the site of a house built in the heyday of Victoria's reign, a house owned by a millionaire with a passion for jewels and a magnificent collection of them.

To that house, when a comparatively young detective-inspector, Bristow had been called . . . From that house a fortune in jewels had been stolen . . . And in that house Bristow had found overwhelming proof that the victim of the theft had been avaricious and cruel, using an age when workers could be exploited and families cheated by a man held high in public esteem. This man, seething and raging, had called on the police to recover his precious hoard, had sacked servants and reviled a son and two daughters for allowing such a sacrilege to happen.

The only clue to the thief was that a man had been seen by a servant, disguised by a blue scarf covering the lower part of his face. All the indications were of a brilliant job of burglary; a then last word in electric alarm systems had been circumvented, safes and strong-room doors blown with consummate skill.

Later, Bristow came to realise that it was the first time he had been on the trail of a man whom Press and public dubbed 'The Baron'. Stories of the prowess of this man soon flew thick and fast; how this Baron, jewel-thief extra-ordinary, robbed the evil rich to pay the worthy poor. Some called him Robin Hood, and as such he had become a legend.

Bristow, at that time the Yard's expert on precious stones, had been the officer assigned to hunting down and capturing this cracksman.

He had failed absolutely.

Bristow, now walking briskly down the hill, decades away in his reverie from the huge red buses lumbering past him, and the stream of cars, had come to realise one morning, with a sense not simply of shock but of astonishment and dismay, that the man known throughout the land as the Baron was a highly reputable man-about-town; a dilettante dabbler in precious stones and small *objets*, named John Mannering.

Gradually, Bristow had committed himself to proving this: it had become not simply his job, but an obsession. Yet the more he had learned about Mannering *alias* the Baron the more he had liked him. He *did* steal from the rich to help the poor. He would take enormous risks to help the exploited or the victimised. He coupled boldness with an unmistakable sense of dedication. As Mannering, he defied Bristow lightheartedly, daring him to find the proof —and there was always a charm about him, an elegance Bristow had to admire.

Bristow had learned more than anyone alive about the Baron; more even than Lorna Fauntley, daughter of Lord Fauntley and as long ago as that a portrait painter of distinction. He had watched their romance, their courtship, their early married life; he had seen Lorna exerting influence on Mannering to make him give up his 'profession', and to this day Bristow was convinced (rightly, it later proved) that it was Lorna who had persuaded him to buy Quinns, one of the most famous antique shops in London: indeed, in all the world.

So much had happened since then.

Time and time and time again Mannering had practised his Baron's craft to help people whom the police could not serve, taking risks for near-strangers that might have led him straight to jail.

Instead of ignominy, however, he had become a consultant to the Yard on jewels and *objets d'art*. One or two Yard officers as well as Bristow held vague suspicions, but no one else *knew* that Mannering and the Baron were one and the same. The relationship between him and Bristow had been quite remarkable, and indeed unique. From a kind of love-hate relationship it had grown to one of deep friendship; and now—and *now* Bristow, ex-Chief Superintendent, was going to manage Quinns in place of Josh Larraby, its manager for many years.

Bristow reached the station at the top of the High Street, and was suddenly confronted by a scraggy woman with silvery hair, who said in shrill tones of horror:

"I never would have thought it, Mr. Bristow!"

She held a white gardenia in her hand; and she looked dumbfounded and distressed as she stared at the flower already in his buttonhole.

"My wife's good luck token, I'm starting a new job," Bristow told her, as briskly as he could. "I couldn't refuse it, could I, Liz?"

The flower seller gasped, then opened her toothless mouth wide.

"No, I s'pose you couldn't. Well there's only one thing to do about it, isn't there?" She placed the gardenia beneath the one already there and pinned it on; and when Bristow proffered her the customary three shillings for it, she pushed his hand away. "Take it with me best wishes, Mr. Bristow." Next moment she was suffused with laughter as she slapped his arm and went on with gusty strength: "Not going on the other side of the fence, are you? Bet you'd lead the cops a pretty song and dance, you would!"

The laughter followed him into the station and down to the platform.

It was a rare morning, too; he got a seat, and glanced in comfort through the *Daily Globe*, not yet used to reading of crimes about which he knew nothing. The headlines seemed to change, so that he read:

The Baron Strikes Again

He chuckled. The words seemed so corny, in retrospect, even bizarre. But they had once been on front pages, and there had been nothing funny or melodramatic about the situation then. He had fought desperately with all the weapons and the strength of Scotland Yard. Time and time again he had been on the point of capturing the man, or of finding absolute proof, but the Baron had always eluded him, and would even taunt: "Better luck next time, Bill." Or: "You'd really hate to catch me, wouldn't you?"

The time had come when Bristow believed that catching the Baron was only a matter of time, for Mannering had taken into his employ at Quinns a man named Larraby, fresh from prison after stealing jewels from the firm for which he had previously worked.

Now *he*, Bristow, was taking Larraby's job; and Larraby had become one of the most respected and most trustworthy men in London.

.   .   .   .   .

Josh Larraby woke early that morning.

He was in the tiny bedroom at the top of Quinns, one of the oldest buildings in the heart of London, an Elizabethan gem, oak-beamed, oak-raftered, with most of the walls of the original wattle, stone and plaster. The room, with its one dormer window which let in plenty of light, held his single bed and a small dressing-table, an upright chair and —near the door where the ceiling was highest—a wardrobe large enough for his three suits, his shirts and ties and collars. Next door was a bathroom, put in when Larraby had moved here to serve as both caretaker and manager. That was over twenty years ago.

Larraby was nearly eighty years old, with snow-white hair and a pink and white complexion, truly an angelic-looking man. He bathed, shaved, and went downstairs to put the finishing touches to the long, narrow shop, the office behind it, and Mannering's own office, to which only he had a spare key.

It was his last working day; a sad, sad day.

He did not think he could have borne it but for the fact that he was still to live here, officially as caretaker although actually—he knew—because Mannering would not make him move away, and Bristow would not try to.

Last day: sad day, nevertheless.

And every piece of furniture, every picture, every piece of jewelled history, every *objet d'art* whether from England or from the other side of the world, must be dusted and made immaculate. He had done much last night, but there was still plenty to do, and he wanted it finished before the young assistants came in at nine o'clock.

Mannering, he felt sure, would be early.

And Bill Bristow was due at half-past nine.

2

QUINNS

Mannering parked his new Aston Martin in a small parking area owned and controlled by the owners and tenants of the shops and flats in or close by Hart Row, Mayfair. On one side of the irregularly-shaped park a concrete-mixer was groaning and clanking, and an outside lift was moving sluggishly up the side of a mammoth new building. This seemed to have been in construction for years but it was in fact only about six months. Stacks of bricks as well as of bags of concrete were neat about the foot of the building, which with its reinforced concrete struts and steel beams and its scaffolding had a skeletal gauntness, even in the bright sunlight. A dozen men worked at the bottom level, others, capped but stripped to the waist, worked at the top. A faint haze of brick and concrete dust was everywhere.

Mannering waved to the workmen who paused to watch him, and they waved back with friendly eagerness. He went out of the car park, through an alley paved with the cobbles of a bygone age. On one side was the oak-beamed, plastered wall of Quinns, there when the alley had first been made; on the other the windowless wall of a row of Georgian houses, all now converted into shops. As the passage debouched into Hart Row, macadam-surfaced now, this contrast between Elizabethan and Georgian was even more apparent. On Quinns' side all the shops were old and beamed and red-tiled, whereas opposite were the taller, graceful Nash-planned buildings.

Quinns was the oldest and the narrowest shop in Hart Row.

Opposite was a milliner's of world renown; a carpet salon; a china shop; an antiquarian bookseller's; a tailor and a small art gallery. On Quinns side were several studio-type buildings and an exclusive photographer. Over the narrow window and the front door of Mannering's shop was written in gold paint and old English lettering, the single word QUINNS.

In the window a single jewelled sword lay on dark blue velvet; and Mannering, seeing it, smiled. For this was a sword once owned by Genghis Khan, a ceremonial sword of the great Mogul Empire which had swept from Russia across a continent and overwhelmed the northern states of India. A few years before, this very sword had been the centre of a series of crimes in which both Mannering and Bristow had been concerned. It was a delightful touch as a welcome for Bristow.

Only Josh Larraby would have thought of it, and been confident enough of himself to put it there.

The shop door opened onto the narrow *salon*, with a strip of Persian carpet down the centre, and each side a treasure house. Small antique pieces, each rare, stood in carefully planned array. On them stood silver caskets or gold, and *objets d'art* selected to match the piece. On the wall were old pictures, including some panels by Breughel. By itself in an alcove was an ikon once owned by Rasputin. Every collector's piece was worthy of a national museum.

And here they were, for sale.

Some were owned by patrons of Quinns, but most were owned by Mannering, who preferred not to be a go-between unless there were special reasons.

Lined up, almost like statues, were the assistants of Quinns.

All of these, except Larraby, who stood at the far end of

the middle passage, rather like a priest with his acolytes about him, were young. They came from families long known to Mannering and were trained both to assist in the shop and to travel the country, buying items for resale. The oldest of these was Lionel Spencer, who was nearest the door. All were dressed in dark suits of the new Edwardian cut, an elegance suggested by Larraby and eagerly followed by the others. Usually these young men would be at work: polishing or cataloguing or poring over the antique dealers' bibles and testaments, checking their knowledge against these books, as they examined a piece of furniture or jewellery or an *objet d'art*.

This way they learned.

There was a constant stream of such young men through Quinns, and many went on from here to management of lesser galleries and shops, or acquired their own in London, or in the country towns frequented by those in search of the beautiful and rare. There was a formidable waiting list of those anxious to replace them.

Today, they were lined up as a reception committee, each reciting as Mannering passed him:

"Good morning, sir."

"Good morning."

"Good morning, sir."

"Good morning."

Their voices were pleasant and subdued but in the expressions of the young men there lurked a glint of humour, each declaring an awareness of the significance of this day.

At last, Mannering reached Larraby.

"Good morning, Josh."

"Good morning, Mr. Mannering."

"Are you trying to frighten Mr. Bristow off?"

"On the contrary, sir, I am attempting to give him a proper welcome."

"Hmm," said Mannering, raising one eyebrow. "I'm not

sure that he wouldn't be better impressed if everyone was doing something. We don't want him to think that we're staffed by stuffed dummies, do we?"

He saw a look of appeal in Larraby's eyes: a kind of: "Don't spoil the joke, sir." And then it dawned on him that this was Larraby's very personal welcome to Bill Bristow: that Larraby, ex-convict, and Bristow, now ex-policeman, merited and would get the same respect from all who worked for Quinns.

"It must be as you wish," Larraby said, quietly.

Mannering grinned at him, his back to the others in the *salon*.

"I'll leave it to you, Josh."

"I do appreciate that, sir. Mr. Bristow should be here in ten minutes. Can you spare me a moment first?"

"Of course," said Mannering. "Come in."

At this far end of the shop behind a Welsh dresser which had been in the same place for years displaying pottery and porcelain, was a parcels counter stacked with everything needed for expert packing. Here, too, were telephones, and a microphone from which any of the assistants could be called, as well as a loudspeaker capable of relaying whatever was being said outside the window of the shop. Many an attempted theft, by violence or stealth and cunning, had been forestalled because the would-be perpetrators had whispered in last moment exhortation or discussion.

Beyond this was the back hall, back door (now about to open onto the new building) and the crooked oak staircase leading up to the storerooms and to Larraby's quarters of bedroom, bathroom, sitting-room and kitchen. On the right was the oak door which led to Mannering's office. He opened the door and ushered Larraby in. This room was small. There was a bow-shaped Queen Anne desk, Mannering's desk, a shelf with reference books at his hand, and above the main chair a portrait of Mannering as a smiling cavalier, painted by Lorna many years before. There were other chairs; noticeably a fine old Regency one. Few people knew that this was fastened to the floor and could only be moved when an electric switch was pulled, for it covered the single entrance to the strong-rooms beneath Quinns. These strong-rooms often held ten times the value of the goods in the showrooms above.

Mannering sat at his desk, and motioned to an upright chair.

"I won't sit just now, sir, thank you," Larraby said. "I just wanted to tell you that everything has been checked thoroughly, the catalogues and records are absolutely up to date—Lionel and I worked yesterday to make sure. And two of the others, Meredith and Sanson, were in most of yesterday, polishing and cleaning."

"Well, well," said Mannering. "I must find a way of thanking them."

"If you'll just let them know you are aware of it that is all the thanks they will need," Larraby assured him. "There is just one other thing."

"What is it, Josh?" asked Mannering.

He studied that strangely youthful face that held more than a touch of a Michelangelo cherub, and the blue eyes which had not faded over the years. He remembered when Larraby had first come to him some twenty years ago, literally then a beggar. And he recalled the prejudice that Bristow had against him, and Bristow's warnings of his folly in placing such a man in a position of trust. Bristow, in those days, had not realised that Larraby's downfall had not been from greed nor even wholly from love of possession. He had stolen jewels because he loved them; he had suffered then as he suffered now, from jewel-mania: an obsessive love of rare and lovely gems.

In a way, so did Mannering.

Now, very slowly, Larraby answered his: "What is it,

Josh?"

"I owe a great deal to Bristow," Larraby said, unexpectedly. "Over the years he changed from downright mistrust to absolute faith, and I can imagine no one whom I would rather see here in my place. But I don't know him, sir, in the sense that you do."

"Are you sure?" asked Mannering, wondering what was coming.

"Quite sure," asserted Larraby. "And because I don't I would be most glad of your guidance. Shall I stay to help him for a week or two: or would it be better for me to leave things entirely to him from the very beginning?"

Now, Mannering understood.

And he was annoyed with himself because he had given no thought to this deeply human problem, and to Larraby's inevitable preoccupation with it. Larraby would still be upstairs, yes, and caretaker, yes: but would he now be forbidden the shop? Would Bristow feel that his own position, as manager, was challenged or at least weakened by having Larraby here all the time? Should he stay in his quarters, away from the shop, lest he be considered interfering?

Larraby looked very anxious.

And Mannering could not be absolutely sure how Bristow would feel.

He knew that Larraby was still acutely conscious of the great gulf between a man who had been in prison and a police officer. They would for ever be on different sides of the fence, no matter how much they liked, or trusted, each other.

"Josh," Mannering said, "I can't be sure, but I think I know the answer."

"And what is it, sir?" Larraby was making a great effort to be detached: but how this issue must matter to him!

"I think that he would soon be lost without you."

Larraby's eyes lit up.

"You *do,* sir?"

"Yes," said Mannering. "I should ration yourself, I think."

"Ration?" echoed Larraby, puzzled.

"Yes. Be available upstairs for a couple of hours each morning and make it obvious you'll be glad to give him any help he needs. And, perhaps, be available for an hour at the end of the day. I think he'll jump at the chance of getting help if he has to ask for it, but hesitate if it's proferred."

"Provided I don't get under his feet all the time," Larraby said with a chuckle. "Thank you, sir. I was a little tensed up about it, and couldn't see clearly. I'm sure you're right. I—"

He broke off, because there was a faint buzz at an internal telephone on Mannering's desk. Mannering picked it up.

"Yes? . . . Oh, good. Thank you." He put down the receiver, and went on to Larraby: "He's turning into the Row."

"I'll be at the door to welcome him," Larraby declared, springing round as lithe as a lad. "Shall I bring him straight to you?"

"Give me a ring," Mannering said, "and I'll come out."

When Larraby had gone, closing the door very quietly, Mannering sat back and pondered. After a while, almost impatient with himself, he opened a file on his desk and began to look through correspondence which Larraby had already opened. The letters would be in order of the importance which Larraby ascribed to them.

The first was a letter signed: *Griselda Leo,* and it was attached to a coloured photograph of some jewels which caught Mannering's eyes as they must have caught Larraby's. The letter read:

Dear Mr. Mannering,

These jewels have come into my possession by a somewhat strange inheritance. Can you tell me if they have any great value? Indeed, if they have any value at all. Needless to say I will bring them to you if you think it would be better to see them.

The address was in Farnham, Surrey.

Mannering studied the photographs.

There were eight pieces: two finger rings, a bracelet, a necklace, two earrings, and two clips. There were diamonds and emeralds, judging from their appearance, and the settings had a quality which was rare in costume pieces. He stretched up to get a book called *Jewellery*—EB–EF—and was about to flip through the pages when the buzzer sounded.

So ex-Superintendent Bristow was here.

* * * *

Bristow turned into Hart Row slowly, at one minute after half-past nine. He felt as if all eyes were turned towards him, whereas probably no one recognised him. The sun was shining down on the whole length of the passage, gilding the cobbles, and he was struck by the beauty of the buildings; the clean Georgian doorways and windows on one side, the old—age-old—buildings on the other.

And he was almost mesmerised by Quinns.

Was this real? Or was it a long-drawn-out dream; an unreality caused by so much thinking, so much obsession, with this shop. Good God! He must have visited it a dozen times to arrest, or at least hoping to charge, John Mannering. And here he was, going to work here!

With old Josh Larraby.

With Mannering.

With some of these young pups who no doubt knew much

more than he about most of the business, for his speciality was jewellery, not furniture or *objets d'art*. As he neared the window, he saw a young policeman, who looked no more than twenty-two or three, approaching along Hart Row. The throb, throb, throb of a distant pile-driver and the metallic clatter of a cement-mixer on the building site beyond, filled the air.

Then he saw the Mogul Sword, and stopped abruptly, staring as if it mesmerised him. Not many years ago, he had actually suspected Mannering of stealing this sword.

He laughed, tension broken, and stretched out his hand for the brass doorknob of Quinns.

3

THE NEW MANAGER

Larraby saw Bristow staring at the Mogul Sword, and for the first time wondered whether he had been wise to put it there. If he had any real reservation about Bristow as a man, it was that he took things too literally: that his sense of humour lacked subtlety; perhaps because he always worked at such pressure.

Then, he saw Bristow's face relax, and a chuckle came over the loudspeaker. Larraby felt great relief as he walked along the Persian carpet to the door. He reached it almost as soon as Bristow.

"*Good* morning, Mr. Bristow."

Bristow gripped the extended hand firmly and, a twinkle in his eyes, responded.

"*Good* morning, Mr. Larraby."

"I'm very glad to see you."

"I'm just trying to make up my mind whether I'm glad to be here," Bristow admitted, ruefully—and then hoped that he hadn't said the wrong thing. He judged from Larraby's expression that he hadn't, and went into the rather shadowy shop, the furniture on either side glowing from centuries of polishing, an occasional piece of jewellery or porcelain shining brightly. Then he saw the young men, standing almost like puppets, and was taken aback. He looked at Larraby suspiciously. Was this a leg-pull?

Mannering came out of his office at the rear of the shop, his face lighting up as he strode forward, hand outstretched.

"Hallo, Bill! It's good to see you!"

"John," said Bristow, "this has been the longest morning I can remember."

"Even longer than those when you came hoping to take me off to jail?" asked Mannering, lightly. There was something so natural in his attitude that the effect of the statuesque young men faded. "We've everybody here so that you can meet them," Mannering went on. "Lionel Spencer you know." Bristow shook hands with a young man who had once made him furiously angry. "John Meredith." Meredith was dark and sallow-faced, lean as a lath with a hand-grip like a vice. "Samuel Sanson and Arthur Rigby." These two young men had overlong but well-groomed hair and healthy complexions; they might have been twins. They gripped firmly but without the bite in Meredith's handshake.

Mannering led Bristow towards the office.

"Come in with us for a few minutes, Josh," Mannering invited, and when they were together in his office, he pointed to the big chair. "Yours, Bill."

"So I guard the strongroom!" Bristow retorted.

"Part of the time. Sit down, Josh." Mannering soon had them reminiscing about their early encounters here, about the fact that they had been on different sides of the fence, and they lost all outward signs of edginess, so skilfully did he put them at their ease. At last, he handed Bristow the letter from Griselda Leo, asking:

"Ever come across anyone named Leo with a private collection of jewels, Bill?"

Bristow pondered.

"I can't say I have, but if we can judge by those settings they're early Victorian, or late Georgian."

"That is exactly my feeling," Larraby put in.

"We'll have them here to look at," said Mannering, and

hitched his chair to the desk. "Josh, why don't you show Bill the stock, and the card index and catalogue systems while I go through the morning's letters?"

Larraby took Bristow out.

Mannering began to go through the letters, which were mostly from England, dealers offering goods for sale, or sending catalogues, but there was a letter from Tusoki, of Tokyo, asking him if he knew where goblets of the Ch'ien Lung period could be found, and one from Rome, enquiring about some early Roman earthenware and porcelain. He made notes about the replies. Either he or Larraby would send the replies, handwritten—

No: he or Bristow. He mustn't forget that!

He sat back in his chair, and laughed aloud: it was an almost incredibly anomalous situation, not far removed from comic. What he should really do was go out and leave Bristow and Larraby to themselves!

He pulled some Quinns letter-heading towards him, a gilded Quinns and the rest of the printing in black on parchment-type paper, and in his flowing hand began to write: *Dear Miss Leo* ...

.   .   .

Bristow, most of his stiffness gone, walked along the aisle, noticing that the young men were now busy, and glad he had put on the darker suit, hot though it was. The tropical weight would have looked too casual. Suddenly, the door opened and the young policeman whom Bristow had seen in the cobbled alley appeared. Bristow happened to be nearest the door, and looked up in mingled surprise and expectancy.

The policeman grinned.

Policemen did *not* grin at a senior officer ...

He wasn't a senior officer at the Yard any more!

"Good morning, sir," the policeman said, happily. "Just looked in to wish you luck at Quinns." The grin became positively gargantuan.

Bristow gulped.

"Er—oh. Thanks." How did this young pup know he had started at Quinns this morning? But he wasn't truly a young pup. He was from Divisional Headquarters at Savile Row, of course; God! The whole of the station must know he was here.

"Anything I can ever do, please let me know," the constable said, and backed out.

Larraby, hiding a smile, remarked: "That was very gracious, wasn't it?"

"Er—yes," said Bristow. "Yes, I—" He broke off. "Do you know I've searched this shop a dozen times, but I've never realised how spick-and-span it is. You must have blessed us when we put our big hands all over everything, and spread grey powder for fingerprints."

"Oh, well," said Larraby, "everyone to his job. I don't know how much Mr. Mannering has told you, but each of our assistants specialises in certain pieces and kinds. Each is trained to general knowledge, but Lionel Spencer for instance specialises in oak furniture of all kinds, and in brass and carvings. We'll have a word with him in a moment. Meredith's especial interest is in jewels and all forms of jewelled—ah—swords and the like." Their eyes met in lively humour. "Sanson's great interest is in porcelain and all forms of pottery, his father was one of the finest collectors of porcelain lions, and in fact all animals, in the world. Rigby—"

The door was flung open so vigorously that Bristow was startled and Larraby looked alarmed. A big and massive man, Quilter of the Yard, so recently one of Bristow's equals and associates, strode in.

"Good lord!" exclaimed Bristow.

"Hallo, Bill," Quilter boomed. "Just looked in to say hallo, and to hope you stay longer in this job than you did in the last."

Bristow had been in the Force thirty years!

Quilter gripped his hand with great power.

"Luck, Bill! Look after him, Josh, and teach him the ways of the wicked!" He clapped Larraby on the shoulder with a force much more apparent than real, then strode out. Bristow almost gaped in his wake.

"Your old friends are very concerned for you," remarked Larraby, and after the briefest of pauses, went on: "As I was saying, Rigby specialises in Regency and Georgian furniture, his ancestral home is Rigby Hall, of course, renowned for its collection of the periods. Do *you* have a particular speciality, Mr. Bristow?"

Bristow looked at him very intently.

"Bill, Josh."

"Eh? Oh. Well, if you prefer—"

"I much prefer you to call me Bill," stated Bristow. "As for my special interest—it's the same as yours."

Larraby drew a deep breath.

"Precious stones."

"In all their glory," Bristow confirmed, and then began to frown. "You know, the more I think about it the more the name 'Leo' rings a bell. There's something about that jewellery. Now if I had access to the records at the Yard—"

He broke off, as the door opened, and under his breath, he said, almost groaning: "Not another."

This was a small, dapper man, followed by a larger, plumper one who carried a camera. The dapper one had once red and now greying hair, a snub nose and rather full lips. He gave a smile as innocent as a babe's, and spoke with obvious satisfaction.

"Hallo, Bill! So you made it! We can't let an occasion

like this pass us without a gossip column piece and a picture, can we?" The plumper man was looking down earnestly into his camera and twisting lenses and breathing hard, while the other, Richard Rackham of the *Globe,* one of London's most successful crime reporters, was smiling his innocent smile and going on: "Is it true that you are going to take over the management from Josh? Or are you really added security? If we could have a picture of the two of you examining a piece suspected of being a fake *or* having been stolen ... Just one more ... That's perfect! ... Is Mr. Mannering in? ... We can't leave the great man out, can we?" Rackham was earnest and facetious at the same time, and when Mannering appeared, summoned by Lionel Spencer, the reporter said warmly: "A great occasion, Mr. Mannering, for all of you. Now if you will stand in between Josh and our William—ah!"

The camera clicked and clicked.

Questions and answers flowed until at last the newspaperman left with his photographer, who had said not a single word. Mannering, Bristow and Larraby, all feeling slightly limp, looked at each other and laughed: and as they laughed a big man with a bald head followed by a girl in her early twenties with the shortest imaginable miniskirt, quite lovely tanned legs, and a camera, came in.

This was 'Tiny' Templeton, of the *Echo.*

"Glad to find you all so cheerful," he said brightly. "Patsy, how about a few pictures now, then—hey, Mr. Mannering! Could you allow our Patsy to go round and take a few photos of your most valuable pieces? Anything worth over four figures will do."

Patsy began snapping and the flashlight blinded all three of the men of Quinns. In next to no time, first Lionel and then each youthful assistant in turn was taking Patsy about the shop, enthusing over each rare specimen, tongues loosened and eyes brightened by her lovely young face. Even

Meredith, at first quite aloof, warmed to her.

"Josh," said Mannering, "prise one of them away if we should get a customer. Meanwhile show Bill what you can of our records." He preceded the others up the aisle, passing the four young men extolling the marvels of Chippendale, their faces lit up by flash after flash. As Mannering turned to go into his office a concealed bell rang out with a note specially contrived to make sure that no one could enter the shop and take the staff unawares.

There, in the shop doorway, stood Chief Inspector, soon to be Superintendent, Gordon, the man who was to succeed Bristow as the Yard's expert on precious stones. A big and rather bony man with pale, gingerish hair, Gordon was usually very straight-faced, but now there was only goodwill on that square, high-cheekboned face.

"Good morning, all," he called. "Good morning, Mr. Mannering. I've just popped in to wish you well."

So they came, throughout the morning. The police and the reporters and the photographers all in good moods, all with apparent goodwill. For Bristow even more than the others it was a crowded day, and not until early afternoon did Larraby go out to use a little of his new freedom. He had not been gone for three minutes before he was back again with a newspaper. Mannering could not remember him being more elated.

"Look!" he said simply, and held out the *Evening Globe*.

There were all three of them at the front of the shop, all excellently portrayed, all smiling happily, men obviously pleased and satisfied with their state and their relationship. But there was more. The photographer who had not said a word but simply gone about his business, had contrived to show the shop itself, foreshortened only a little and in no way distorted. There were all the lovely pieces of furniture, some of the paintings, and the *objets* shown with a kind of texture which was rare in any photography and not far from unique in a newspaper.

Mannering could not have been more pleased.

"I'll telephone and get some prints," he said. "This really will be a souvenir of a great day. And we need some copies of this newspaper. Samuel—"

"I'll get them, sir, and bring them back," promised Larraby.

When he had gone, there was a lull in callers, except for two Americans, one Japanese and an Irishman, all interested in the Mogul Sword—or so they said. They were more interested in Mannering and Bristow, Mannering suspected. Towards five o'clock, after Larraby had come back with the newspapers, and Tiny Templeton and his Patsy had gone, there was something near normality at Quinns. Soon a Yorkshireman, roughly dressed and looking uncomfortably sweaty and hot, came in and asked if they had any silver chalices by Cellini.

In the strong-room, there were two.

Larraby took Bristow down to get them, and the Yorkshireman, bluff of face and manner, took one look at them and another at Mannering.

"How much?" he asked.

"For the smaller—" Mannering began.

"For them both," the Yorkshireman said.

"Seventeen thousand three hundred and fifty pounds," stated Mannering flatly.

"I'll take them," declared the Yorkshireman, with hardly a pause for breath. "I'll give you my cheque now and call in on Wednesday to collect them, Mr. Mannering." He took a dog-eared cheque book from his pocket, wrote the cheque to Quinns with a cheap ballpoint pen, said: "Good day to you," and departed.

Bristow gaped after him.

"If they are all as easy as that—" he began, and then broke off, knowing that sales were seldom as easy as that, and marvelling at the calm way in which Mannering and Larraby took the swift deal. There was some evidence of excitement among the younger men, at least, so they were not entirely sated by such signs of opulence.

"I think we'll call it a day," said Mannering.

But it was not a day fated to end with such a summary decision. While he was speaking, and while Samuel Sansom was smoothing his hair, obviously eager to go, the front door opened with its almost ominous *clang!* and Gordon came in, a little more aggressive and a little less amiable than before.

"I was passing so I thought I'd look in rather than telephone," he said. "About those jewels associated with the name of Leo, Bill. Remember, you asked me if they rang a bell."

"Yes?" said Bristow, suddenly tense; as indeed, were Larraby and Mannering.

"Well they didn't then, but they do now," Gordon went on. "They're part of the Ottenshaw Collection stolen in 1960 and never recovered. If they are the McCoy, we need to know quickly."

And he stared at Bristow as if accusing Bristow himself of being ready to keep evidence from the police.

4

CLASH OF LOYALTIES?

"Well, well," said Bristow, very lightly. "So I have a crime on my hands on my first day here." He glanced at Mannering with a comical expression on his face, which was puckered as if in bewilderment. Suddenly, he threw up his hands, and faced Mannering squarely. "I'm going to need briefing from you on this, John. Do we co-operate with the police or do we find out what we can on our own?"

"We co-operate to the full," Mannering said earnestly.

"Just as we always have," murmured Larraby, wickedly.

"If you're having me on—" began Gordon.

"Don't be an ass, Ian," Bristow interrupted, in a brisk voice. "Why on earth should we have you on? And we asked you if you knew anything, didn't we? Now you've given us something to go on we have to decide what to do next."

"Precisely," said Mannering, still earnestly.

"Under your guidance," said Larraby, so meek-sounding, so angelic-looking and so wicked-meaning.

Gordon looked at them in turn, suspiciously, giving a strange impression of a man at bay. Finally his gaze came to rest on Bristow, and he asked gruffly:

"Well? What will you do?"

"I know what I'd like to do," said Bristow.

"What's that?"

"Have a look at the Yard's files on the Ottenshaw job, check all that was stolen, and everything we—I mean the

Yard—did. Next I'd go and see this woman who calls her-self Leo and have a look at the jewels. If they're genuine and they're stolen property, then I'd make an official re-port." Bristow turned to Mannering on his last words and asked almost in defiance: "Wouldn't you, John?"

"It depends," demurred Mannering.

"What do you mean—it depends? Depends on what?" demanded Gordon, now openly glowering.

"On the woman," Mannering said. "I would want to find out whether she knew they were stolen. I'd like to know what she means in her letter, especially what she means by the phrase 'a rather strange inheritance'. Then if it seemed necessary I would advise her to go to the police."

"What you really mean is that if you thought she was in trouble you'd help her, whether she had a legal right to the jewels or not."

Mannering's manner, mild and pleasant until then, sud-denly changed. Gordon's almost angry glare was met by a look of cold hostility, and even Gordon was taken aback: he looked positively abashed. Bristow obviously marvelled at the change; at the new hardness in Mannering's ex-pression as he said:

"There have been times and will be more when people are more important to me than the police. I would—I *will* check as fully as possible and then decide on a course of action."

Larraby smiled slightly, while Bristow's face showed no expression. Young Sam Sanson, the only one of the assist-ants within earshot, made a great show of cleaning a piece of Dresden porcelain: three dancers, pirouetting.

At last Gordon said: "No offence meant, Mr. Mannering. I'm a straightforward copper, you know, I haven't got the finesse or the experience of Mr. Bristow." He smiled thinly. "Last thing I want is to get him off to a bad start. Promise me one thing, will you?"

Mannering, surprised and almost contrite, answered warmly: "If I possibly can."

"Consult us if you think there's any monkey business. Keep us in the picture. No one at the Yard is ever going to think Bill Bristow had changed sides, but sometimes *you* do some bloody funny things." He looked alarmed again, as if afraid that his forthrightness would cause offence, but his face cleared as Mannering chuckled.

"That's an understatement, if ever there was one. If this proves a job for the police, I'll certainly tell you."

"It would be the Farnham—the Surrey—chaps," Bristow put in.

"The Ottenshaw robbery was in Regent's Park, so it's ours too," Gordon observed shrewdly. "Tell you what," he went on with obvious eagerness, "come and have a pint and see what you remember about the job."

He meant: I'll jog your memory with the help of Records.

"Good idea," Mannering said.

So on his first day at Quinns, Bristow left with the man who had been his chief *aide* at the Yard for years. Gordon, half-a-head taller and half as well dressed, turned to raise a hand as he reached the door. Mannering went to his office, while Larraby saw the younger men off the premises and locked up; Bristow's job, in future. The locks, once in place, were electronically secured, and a burglar alarm system flashed a warning in the offices of one of the big private security firms. Mannering knew better than to think Quinns was burglar-proof, but it was as nearly so as a shop could be.

He pressed a button in his desk, and the Regency chair moved; another button, and part of the parquet floor slid beneath the wall, revealing a flight of steps leading down to the strong-room. There were four sections. He placed the two Cellini caskets in a safe in the first section and went back, locked up, and was looking at the Yorkshireman's cheque when Larraby tapped at the door.

"Come in, Josh," Mannering called, and the door opened immediately. "You must be exhausted," he remarked. "It wasn't exactly a restful day."

"But a fascinating one, sir."

"Reassured about Bristow's attitude?" asked Mannering, and to his surprise Larraby hesitated for a moment, looking very preoccupied. Mannering did not urge him to answer, but waited, until Larraby said:

"In a way, sir."

"What aren't you sure about?"

"Well—" Larraby hesitated, and then his lips puckered and his eyes twinkled. "I'm hoist with my own petard in one way, Mr. Mannering. Bristow would always say 'once a thief, always a thief', and I wouldn't doubt that he wonders about me sometimes. I'm quite sure Gordon does! And I— ah—I find myself thinking 'once a policeman always a policeman'. If you follow me, sir."

"I follow you closely," Mannering assured him. "If I took chances over this case or any other, Bristow might feel he had to play by police rule and regulation."

"I do wonder, sir," Larraby admitted.

"You know the truth, don't you?" Mannering mused. "I am always likely to take chances, and if Bill Bristow had to play by the rules in every case, then our relationship wouldn't work out. I do realise it, Josh."

"As I am sure you have all along, sir," said Larraby. "I think the possibility very remote, mind you."

"But it exists," Mannering said. "Thanks, Josh. Well, I'll get home. There's a re-run of *Romeo and Juliet* at the Academy, and I've promised to take Lorna."

While Mannering and Lorna were watching the tapestry-soft beauty of the film *Romeo and Juliet*, Bristow watched a television play, which saved him from talking much to his wife. When he had come home she had asked:

"Did the day go all right, dear?"

"Very good indeed," Bristow had assured her.

So used was she to quelling her curiosity, if indeed she felt any, that she made no further reference. Bristow pondered all that Gordon had told him of the Ottenshaw robbery. A private collection of jewels had been stolen, the police had been called in within an hour of the discovery of the theft, but had found no clue, no trace of the men who, judging from the signs, had broken in.

"I had a word with Percy Bush," Gordon had told him. "He was a detective officer at the time, at the place. He and the other police thought it was an inside job; there was a wastrel son and a lot of family feud stuff. Never found a jewel, not a single one."

And then Gordon had paused, and looked Bristow very straight in the eyes.

"If these things the Leo woman has got are part of the collection, the other stuff might be around, too. It's an unsolved crime, Bill. If it comes to a showdown, you wouldn't take a chance and keep material facts from us, would you? You could get yourself into a lot of trouble if you did."

"Don't I know it," Bristow had replied, noncommittally. Ever since that discussion, he had been pondering.

In theory, of course, he had known that he might come face to face with questions of conscience, but he hadn't expected to run into anything like this on his first day. And it was useless to tell himself that this was probably a perfectly straightforward case without any criminal overtones. Even if it proved to be, the fact had to be faced: if Mannering decided to take the law into his own hands, then he, Bristow, would have to take his side or the law's.

One didn't stop being a policeman simply by retiring.

Suddenly, he said aloud: "I wonder what I would do if it came to the crunch?"

His wife looked up from a romantic novel she was reading while half-watching television.

"What was that, dear?"

"Oh, nothing," said Bristow, and she turned back to her book. But to himself he went on: If I had to jump on to the Yard's side I couldn't keep on working at Quinns.

Now he began to wonder for the first time whether he should have taken the job. He was not yet perturbed, just slightly uneasy. For if the woman Leo proved to be in trouble, then nothing he or the Yard could do would prevent Mannering from trying to help her, whether it meant breaking the law or not.

He wished he knew more about Griselda Leo.

    ·   ·   ·   ·

Griselda Leo looked across at the elderly man who was in the kitchen with her, without speaking. She was still young, thirty-ish perhaps, but her forehead was furrowed as if with worry and anxiety. She wore no make-up except for a touch of lipstick which was too purple for her pale face. Her black hair was drawn straight back from her forehead and tied in a pony tail. She had quite remarkable eyes, black but luminous, not opaque-seeming as were most dark eyes.

She looked a little scared.

"Griselda," the man said. "You've got the money, I know you have."

"No I haven't, Ted," she denied.

"Come off it, dearie—I only need a pony—fifty pounds, I mean."

"You mean a pony," she said with weary certainty. "And

you want it to put on a horse which you're sure will win
and—"

"And it *will* win!" cried the elderly man, her uncle. "It's
an absolute certainty for the two-thirty at Salisbury tomorrow. It just can't lose." His grey eyes were radiant as if
with pre-knowledge, his whole face lit up. "And it's
twenty-five to one! I'll be able to pay you back all I owe
you, and—"

"*No,* Ted."

"But Grizzy, it's a certainty!"

"There isn't such a thing as a racing certainty," argued
Griselda, "and even if there were, I couldn't lend you any
more, because I haven't got any."

Ted's radiance faded, and he spoke sulkily, looking down
at his feet.

"You're lying to me, and you know it."

"I'm not," Griselda said wearily. "I won't have a five
pound note until Friday, when I get paid."

". . . lying to your own flesh and blood," Ted was mutter-
ing.

She caught her breath, and something in her change of
manner affected her uncle, who drew back as if in alarm.
Griselda sprang to her feet and snatched a cup and saucer
from the table.

"Don't call me a liar! Do you understand? *Don't ever
call me a liar again.* All my life I've been plagued by you,
tormented by you. I don't owe you a thing. I haven't any
responsibility for you, I don't have to feed you and find
room for you whenever you're so broke you can't go anywhere else. I don't owe you a thing, do you hear?" She
brandished the cup and some of the dregs splashed, onto
the table and onto him. "If you ever call me a liar again
I'll throw you out. I'm tired of it—tired of going short while
you throw your money away on gambling and drink. *My
God!*" she screamed. "I never see you if you back a win-

ner. I only see you when you're stony-broke and hungry. Well, I'm finished with you, understand? If it weren't for you I'd have thousands of pounds, instead of that I've hardly saved a penny. I may have owed my father something, but you—I don't owe you a thing. And I'll never lend you—*lend?* that is a laugh—another penny, not as long as I live. Do you understand? I'm through with you!"

He sat beneath this tirade, eyes enormous, whole face showing both surprise and despair. He did not speak. When she swung away and rushed out of the little dining alcove into the kitchen, he simply stared at her, like a child hurt but not understanding.

When she came back, he had gone to the spare room, no more than a box-room. She could see the light beneath his door, and hear radio music playing softly. Whenever she was angry with him, he would keep the radio tuned very low. When he thought she had recovered, he would turn it up a little, but never enough for the neighbours to complain.

Tonight, she had been much angrier than she had ever known herself, and she felt no softening of mood towards him. She did not call out to say good night, but went to her own crowded room, the room of relics of furniture and photographs, and went to a chiffonier, a beautiful piece of Elizabethan oak which had a secret drawer. She pressed a piece of the carving, a tiny section of a sword held in a soldier's hand, and the drawer was released. She pulled it open with her fingers, slowly so as not to break her nails.

Winking up at her were the jewels she had written to John Mannering about. She looked at them for a long time, then hid them away in a different hiding place, this time behind the right-hand door of a corner cupboard.

5

FORTUNE IN FURNITURE

Bristow felt a different man next morning.

A good night's sleep had set most of his anxieties and apprehensions at rest, and he whistled on his way to the front door, the morning's newspapers and the post. There were two brief notes, from friends, wishing him well at Quinns, and a letter from Ethel's mother. Perhaps she wanted her daughter to spend a few weeks with her in the country. His heart leapt, and immediately he felt mean. He spread out *The Times* and the *Daily Globe*, the two extremes of national dailies; and was astounded.

In *The Times* there was a good photograph of Mannering and himself standing by one of the paintings and a Sheraton table. In the *Globe* there was a whole middle page spread, with a photograph of him standing with Mannering and Larraby, and several of the shop. The captions read:

FORTUNE IN FURNITURE—1
An Italian Pietra Dura: £15,000

FORTUNE IN FURNITURE—2
A William & Mary Oyster Cabinet worth £17,500

Beneath the last picture ran the story, centred, and in bold type. The headline ran:

WHAT TURNS £60 into £17,500?

ANSWER ... OLD AGE!

Bistow read the story thoroughly. The *Globe* had gone back to the year of manufacture and showed a photograph of an old, beautifully inscribed, bill:

To wood and materials	£27. 10s. 8d.
To labour of craftsman (7 weeks)	£21. 11s. 4d.
To labour of apprentices	
James Leeson (8 weeks)	£ 1. 15s. 0d.
T. Wall	£ 1. 15s. 0d.
William Golightly	£ 1. 8s. 0d.
To hire of carriages & carts	£ 2. 1s. 4d.
To etceteras	£ 3. 17s. 2d.
	£59. 18s. 6d.

There was a scrawled signature, obviously the receipt. The article ran:

Look at the bill of costs for a typical piece of furniture made about 280 years ago. Then look at the photograph on the right, above. That is at Quinns, famed London antique dealers, owned by John Mannering. Its price: £17,500!

What has increased the value?

Age—and rarity.

It is said there are only three of these beautiful pieces of furniture in the world. One: at Buckingham Palace. One: at the Mellon Gallery in Washington. One: at Quinns.

Our reporter asked John Mannering how he reached the asking price. 'By comparing the prices asked and paid for pieces not identical but not dissimilar. And by checking with such auctioneers as Sotheby's and Christies.'

The truth is, these pieces of age-plus-rarity are beyond price.

Mr. Mannering could ask three, four, five times as much and get it from a collector.

But Mr. Mannering says: 'I shall make a fair profit, and I don't ask more.'

Many dealers would say this but not mean it. Mr. Mannering means it. He is the antique dealer who once bought an Old Master for £25, sold it for £15,000 and sent half of this to the original owner, a Cornish fisherman.

That speaks very well for John Mannering.

See the other thing which speaks well for him? The man at the left of the trio above? That is ex-Superintendent William Bristow, until a month ago the ace detective at Scotland Yard.

Now he has retired. Yesterday, he started work at Quinns.

We hope Mr. Mannering gives him a share of any profits made over deals which ex-Superintendent Bristow makes. Because he will deserve it.

Who is the white-haired, venerable figure on the right of the picture? That is the retiring manager of Quinns, Joshua Larraby. It is said that next to John Mannering, Larraby probably knows more about precious stones than anyone else in the world.

In the middle of the picture: handsome John Mannering himself.

Millionaire?

He won't admit it but he almost certainly is!

As he read, Bristow made tea, and when he took it into the bedroom, he spread the *Daily Globe* out for his wife to read then hurried out. On the way to Quinns, he wondered what Mannering would think of the article.

＊ ＊ ＊

Mannering and Lorna, one with *The Times* and one with the *Daily Globe*, read with fascinated interest.

"Darling," said Lorna, suddenly, "you would let me know if you were a millionaire, wouldn't you?"

"The only way I can possibly find out is to ask the newspapers," Mannering replied.

The middle page spread was read all over London, from West to East End, in trains and in buses and at breakfast tables. Almost every policeman in London read it, those who took the *Daily Globe* sharing it with their colleagues, as well as almost every criminal who had been charged by Bill Bristow. So did every jewel thief, and every antique dealer. Even Griselda Leo, on her way to the bookshop where she worked.

When Bristow reached Quinns at nine-fifteen that morning, the normal opening time, he saw a crowd at the end of Hart Row, and as he pushed his way through, saw that the whole street was thronged, and the cobbled passage was choc-a-bloc with sightseers. The thump-thump-thump of the pile driver and the clatter and rattle of the cement-mixer sounded above the noises. Larraby was at the door of the shop, inside, looking baffled. There was a sharp hoot of a car horn and Bristow, now one of the crowd, turned to see Mannering's Aston Martin, flanked by two policemen, moving slowly into the street. Mannering was smiling, as if enjoying himself.

Then Bristow saw a man he knew as Locky Cartwright; and, near him, a smaller man named Lewis, both of them expert safe-breakers and jewel-thieves, both of whom he had put inside. Cartwright, not unlike Gordon to look at, had the nerve to wave. Then Lewis, a man with enormous head, hands and feet, looked at him and said:

"Jumped out of the frying pan into the fire, haven't you, Bill?"

"You stay in the pan," retorted Bristow good-humouredly.

More police arrived and the crowd, mostly people on their way to work intrigued by what they had read, thinned out. Bristow and Mannering, now in the shop, examined the two pieces which had caused such a sensation. Then Bristow and Larraby began the work they had started on yesterday, but they had hardly got under way before the door opened with more of a clang than normal, and a man came in.

He was broad across the shoulders and very thick-set. He wore a short black beard, and had a crop of thick, wiry hair. His eyebrows were black too, and under them his grey eyes seemed to be the colour of silver.

He stood four-square in the aisle, the closed door behind him, and Bristow moved slowly forward.

There was something forbidding, menacing, about the bearded man. His very stillness emphasised this. He had a reputation known to everyone here; and he was a man who could strike fear into many. At the back of the shop, Larraby moved quietly to Mannering's office, and tapped. Mannering had to get up and unlock the door.

"What is it, Josh?"

"Black Knight is here," stated Larraby simply.

Mannering replied, in a tone which seemed to reject what he had been told: "Black *Knight*?"

"Beyond doubt, sir," Larraby confirmed.

Mannering went into the shop, seeing Bristow facing the man who had entered. There was utter stillness, until Lionel Spencer moved towards him on one side, and John Meredith on the other.

"Do you need help?" asked Meredith.

"Shall we throw him out?" whispered Spencer.

"I don't think it will come to that here," Mannering said. "But stand by."

"Who is he?" asked Spencer, puzzled but affected by the general mood.

"An old enemy," Mannering answered softly, and went forward to join Bristow. After a moment or two, he broke the long silence but not the tension. It was as if the man whom Larraby called 'Black Knight' had brought danger with him: had come deliberately to spread fear. "Well, Black," he said in an even voice, "when did you get out of prison?"

"Two weeks ago," the man answered.

His voice was somehow a disappointment, not as deep as his figure and his strong features promised; but it did not detract from the menace; and the slow way in which he spoke was impressive.

"Two weeks," repeated Mannering. "Where have you been?"

"Two weeks, after ten years inside," Black Knight went on. "Ten years."

"You could have served twenty," Mannering said sharply.

"You certainly deserved to," said Bristow drily.

"Just the same swine, aren't you?" Black Knight said. "And that goes for both of you."

"What do you want?" demanded Mannering quietly.

"I just wanted to see the pair of you together in the flesh," sneered Knight. "And I've brought news for you."

"What news?"

"Money's no use to a dead millionaire."

"That's enough—" Bristow began.

"Or to a dead ex-copper," sneered Knight. "I'm going to kill you both."

"Just saying that, uttering threats and menaces, could get you back in jail and they wouldn't let you out in a hurry," Bristow said roughly.

"*You* won't ever put me back in jail," Knight declared. "You're not a copper any longer. You won't be anything much longer. Nor you." The uncanny-looking silvery eyes turned towards Mannering. "Beautiful things you've got here, Mannering. I'm going to burn them up in front of your eyes."

He stood with his hands a little in front of his waist, as if oblivious of the fact that Meredith on one side and Spencer on the other were drawing closer, neither of them frightened by his size and obvious strength. The other two assistants, and Larraby, were still at the back of the shop.

"I really shouldn't try," Mannering said.

"Well, you're not me," retorted Knight. "You haven't spent ten years rotting in jail because a copper and a copper's nark turned you in. If it weren't for you two, I'd have been out of the country. I was going to South America —the Argentine. I had a nice little hacienda ready and a woman who knew all about pleasing a man. It was all there, sitting pretty—and instead of going there I spent half my time in Dartmoor and half at Wormwood Scrubs. Now life looks good to you two, but you're going to know what it's like to have it snatched away from you. Don't ever think you'll get away from me. They won't even hang me for killing you, these days: but even if they would, I would still get you."

He looked as if he meant every word, and was perfectly capable of carrying out his threat.

Meredith and Spencer were now between him and the door, ready to stop any attack, prepared to leap at him at the slightest threatening move. Spencer said tersely:

"Shall we hold him, Mr. Mannering?"

"Or get the police?" Meredith suggested.

Mannering said something which astounded them all. In an impatient, testy way, he replied:

"No. If he wants to, let him come and talk to me in the

office."

And he turned his back on the man Black Knight, as if deliberately asking for trouble. The youngsters gasped: Larraby closed his eyes. Bristow, so much smaller than the man in front of him, shifted his position slightly.

"Mannering!" Knight called.

Mannering walked steadily on.

"*Mannering!* Come back or I'll put a bullet in your back."

Mannering did not show any sign that he had heard, but reached the door and opened it, then stared along the aisle. There was Knight, glowering, right hand thrust forward and a small pistol in it. If he fired he could hardly miss Mannering, who stood still, calling coldly:

"You deserved all you got."

"Why, you—"

"But you're still a young man," Mannering said.

"*Young!* Every year inside is like ten out!"

"You're not much past thirty-five," Mannering insisted. "You're as fit as you ever were. If you don't play the fool you can enjoy living. If you cause any trouble here, you'll end up in jail before you really know what it's like to be free. When you come out next time you won't be young any longer."

He stayed there, just long enough for the words to sink in, then went into the office. There was no sound; no zutt! such as the automatic would make. He sat down, listening; there was no movement for a few seconds, until suddenly there were heavy footsteps, the clang of the door being opened, another as it closed.

He sat back in his chair, sweating.

In the shop, it was as if everyone had been released from a tension which held them taut. There were more movements, footsteps, voices as they talked to one another. Then Bristow appeared at the doorway, very pale.

"My God," he said. "I thought he was going to shoot

you."

"And set fire to the place?" asked Mannering.

"He's quite capable of it. You must know that, John."

"Yes, I know," Mannering agreed. "But we got through that crisis and we'll get through any others, one by one. Bill, did you fool yourself into thinking that this job might be a sinecure?" He was smiling faintly.

"No," replied Bristow, slowly, "but I didn't think it would be like this, either. John—you should ask the Yard to have Knight followed. I think you should charge him with uttering threats and menaces. He would go back for at least three years."

"Possibly, and come out more vindictive than ever." Before Bristow could answer, Mannering went on: "Bill, I want you to take over today, I'm going out to Farnham. I'll look in at antique shops in the area and call on Griselda Leo some time after six."

He pushed his chair back and stood up, as if there had been no threats from Black Knight, no hint of danger.

6

GRISELDA LEO

The *Daily Globe* and *The Times* had done their work well. Wherever Mannering went he was recognised and in most of the shops he called on, prices went up from the normal in a way which, a few years ago, would have angered him. Now, he took it almost for granted, and perhaps was over-pleased when, in a small shop in Farnham, near the Borough with its graceful Georgian houses, a young man with a spade-shaped beard offered a Gougon lion at a hundred guineas.

"And very cheap at the price, Mr. Mannering!"

Mannering fingered the markings on the lion, and hesitated. He did not specialise in bronzes although there was a rising market both at home and overseas.

"If it will make the difference," the bearded man said, "I'll settle for ninety. I don't mind admitting I've had a

bad week. There haven't been many people in the shop, and last weekend I sold three hundred pounds' worth of glass and porcelain on the strength of a credit card and an honest face. The cheque bounced."

"Oh, bad luck," Mannering said. "All right, I'll take the lion. Do you have a box?"

"Of course." The young man took a box from a corner; it was already filled with tissue paper, and he rearranged this and placed the bronze in with great care. "Phew!" he exclaimed as he finished, looking at Mannering with a curiously boyish expression. "I feel better now. It was like being visited by royalty!"

"Oh, nonsense!"

"It isn't nonsense," declared the young man. "If my father were here he'd swoon! He lives in Birmingham, though—was here last week for a holiday." He finished fastening the box with tape, signed a receipt with the name Frank Goodman, and then asked: "Anything else, sir?"

"Not in sight," said Mannering.

"If there's anything you would like me to look out for—" the other suggested, hopefully.

"If there is, I'll let you know," said Mannering with skilful evasion, and picked up the box. Then he asked casually: "By the way, where is the Borough?"

"Just along on the right," Goodman replied. "Do you want any place in particular?"

"Number 47d," said Mannering.

The young man's expression changed from one of hope deferred to one which might be of concern. Certainly it was a reaction Mannering could not have anticipated. He waited, while the other obviously collected his thoughts, and doing so he realised that this was not a bright and breezy young man who said the first thing that came into his head, but one who considered first, and then spoke with an air of assumed simplicity.

"Do you mean Griselda Leo's flat?"

"Yes," answered Mannering, looking astonished. "Do you know her?"

"Every antique and second-hand dealer in the area knows her," stated the young man. "She was in here only a few days ago, trying to sell me a piece of Worcestershire pottery. One of the loveliest figurines ever to come out of the Midlands. It was worth all of two hundred pounds and I simply couldn't afford to pay the money. I offered to try to sell it for her but she was in a hurry. God knows what she got for it. Some damned shyster probably paid her twenty or twenty-five."

"Did you tell her how much you thought it was worth?" asked Mannering.

"Oh, yes."

"Wouldn't she be guided by you?"

"I don't think she would be guided by any man, she doesn't trust the sex." Goodman pursed his lips. "And I can't say I blame her. But she was probably in urgent need of money and would sell it for any cash she could get."

"You make her sound very intriguing," remarked Mannering.

"In a way she is," replied Goodman.

"How well do you know her?"

"Oh, fairly well as an acquaintance. I don't know her well socially. As a matter of fact I met her first some years ago. My wife was alive then." He stared out of the window, but soon looked back at Mannering, his blue eyes shadowed as if by memory. "She lived in the whole house then. Now she's living in a few rooms upstairs—the old attic, the servants' quarters—and she flogs everything she ever had. I went into that house once, years ago," went on Goodman. "I'm not exaggerating, Mr. Mannering. That place was a treasure house. Now it's turned into flats, four altogether, and you'd never recognise it. What's left of the treasure is squeezed into her flat, at the top. Some tenants—" He broke off, frowned, then seemed to draw himself to attention. "But I shouldn't be standing here gossiping. Do you mind if I ask you a question?"

"Go ahead."

"Why are you going to see Griselda Leo?"

"She asked me to," said Mannering simply.

"You mean she's got something she thinks you—" Goodman broke off with a sharp snap of his fingers. "It's none of my business. I'm sorry. You'll find Number 47 at the far end of the Borough, surrounded by a dilapidated brick wall. The door to her flat is at the back, you'll see the number on it: 47d."

"Thank you," Mannering said. "You've been most helpful."

He picked up the bronze and went out. A policeman was coming towards his car, parked on a yellow line longer than he had intended. He put the box in the boot and straightened up as the policeman, middle-aged and very fit and strong-looking, approached him.

"Hallo," Mannering said. "Have I been law-breaking?"

The policeman looked at him very intently.

"Strictly speaking yes, sir, but if you're just off, that's all right."

"Thank you," said Mannering, and then saw the other's expression brighten as recognition dawned.

"You *are* Mr. Mannering, aren't you?"

"That's right."

"Glad to know you, sir!" the policeman said. "I was reading about you in *The Times* this morning. As a matter of fact it was Mr. Bristow who interested me most. He was down here on a case a few years ago. I was a rookie, then, and had the pleasure of watching him work. *Very* instructive, sir—proper object lesson as a matter of fact."

"But he didn't inspire you to transfer to the C.I.D.?"

"I was tempted to try, sir, but I played safe."

"Probably wise," said Mannering. He was aware of Goodman standing in the small, bow-shaped window of his shop and of people standing on the other side of the street staring at him. "What case was that?" he asked.

"Burglary, over at Tilford House," the policeman answered. "You might give Mr. Bristow my regards, sir. Police Sergeant Nebb. Nebb, sir. He won't remember, of course, but—"

"Bill Bristow has a remarkable memory," Mannering

said. "I'll tell him."

He drove off, trying to remember details of the Tilford House robbery. The house, between this old town and Guildford, was a show place, and its gardens were opened to the public at weekends. He knew of the robbery but the details were so blurred that he put it out of his mind. It may well have happened when he was out of the country.

He turned left, into the wide thoroughfare called the Borough. There was ample parking on either side and cars were pulling out; it might already be six o'clock. He saw the dilapidated brick wall, a few yards on the left, and saw the number 47 written in faded black on weathered white of a wooden, five-barred gate. The gate stood open and there was room to drive in but he parked close to the wall from which once-white paint or wash had flaked off in patches.

As he walked, he saw what was far too common in the English countryside: a garden that had once been lovely, but was now neglected and overgrown. Weeds strewed the carriageway and there had been no new gravel down for years. Rose beds were overgrown with weeds, their dying buds wizened and undersized. The front door had been painted by a casual and slapdash amateur. Two small children, one with a dummy in a cupid's bow mouth, stood by a low window and stared at him.

He went round to the back.

Someone had dug and developed a vegetable patch, which stood, strangely incongruous, in a wilderness of long grass, thistles, purple nettles and sweet peas run wild. One huge rambler, most of it unproductive briar, covered a broken-down fence.

One thing stood out: the narrow door on which was marked: 47d. It was freshly painted, and the step was white and clean, the brass surround of the bell push gleamed. He pressed it. There was no immediate response, which didn't surprise him now that he knew that Griselda Leo lived at the top of the house. Soon he heard footsteps, and the door opened.

A young woman stood there.

Her hair was drawn tightly back from her forehead in a pony tail. She wore no make-up, except rather too much lipstick. Her eyes were big and dark, with something of the half-frightened look of a fawn. She wore a simple dress, apple green in colour, with short sleeves.

"Good evening," said Mannering.

"Good evening," she said, without the slightest sign of recognition.

"Miss Griselda Leo?"

"Yes, I—*oh!* You're Mr. Mannering!"

"Yes," said Mannering.

"Oh, my goodness," she said in sudden confusion. "I had your letter this morning but I didn't expect—oh dear. I haven't had any time to tidy up, I'm afraid, I had such a trying day and—" She broke off in dismay, and only slowly became aware that he was smiling at her.

"It doesn't matter a bit," he said, "provided I can see the jewels?"

"Oh, well—yes, of *course*. But—oh, please come in." As she stood aside to let him pass, she added in the now familiar tone of apology: "I'm sorry about the stairs, they're rather narrow. Shall I lead the way?"

"Please," said Mannering—and almost gaped. The back staircase was circular, with a beautifully shaped banister and slender uprights. And the wall was panelled with a gracefulness one seldom saw. At each of three landings windows were let into the thick wall, each window arched with exquisite line. This was a gem: and this was the old servants' entrance! What must the main staircase be like!

They reached the last landing, and even up here the walls were panelled and the four doors leading off had the graciousness of the early Georgian period. She opened the second door on the left, and as Mannering went in he saw that one door was ajar; and a man stood at it, eyes very bright. He showed no sense of embarrassment at being seen, just stood staring.

The room into which Mannering was led, had a low ceiling and small windows but the same lovely proportions as everything he had seen here. But the contents, far more than the room itself, astounded him. Excepting a small group of chairs, every item of furniture was worthy of space at Quinns. Lionel Spencer would have drooled over the Jacobean chiffonier, with spare, delicate carving and a beautiful colour which could only have been acquired with centuries of polishing. The periods were mixed up, but a glance was enough to tell him that there were four Chippendale, and two William and Mary chairs, and a Sheraton sofa table. There was a small refectory table, too, and on it several vases which he felt sure were early Japanese. On the mantelpiece and on the furniture which was obviously not in regular use were other pieces of china. Exquisite miniatures appeared to be fastened round the fireplace by tin-tacks.

Griselda Leo watched him tensely.

"I *am* sorry it's such a mess. Please—please sit down."

He sat down, rather gingerly, in a Chippendale masterpiece, noting again her nervousness, and the fact that she was very much on edge. He waited for her to speak, and across the silence came a creak of sound at the door.

Quite suddenly, he sprang up and pulled the door open wide. A frail-looking elderly man with a pale, lined face stood there.

"Ted!" the girl cried in tones of despair. "Ted! I told you to go."

'Ted' did not seem to notice her, but looked intently at Mannering. There was no doubt of the cunning in his eyes.

His lips were moist and quivery, his hands unsteady.

"I wanted to make sure you were all right," he said.

"If you don't go away—" she began on a note of resigned anger.

"It's not right, entertaining a strange man in your flat alone," stated the old man. "It's just not right."

The girl stood in front of him, her hands clenched and raised, and her lips working. Mannering thought: at any moment she is going to burst into tears. But she did not. Without the slightest warning she leapt forward and flung herself bodily at the old man. She began to beat him about the shoulders and chest, using her arms like flails, and he backed away, making ineffectual efforts to protect himself.

The door was wide open.

Before Mannering could reach them, Griselda Leo had pushed the man into the narrow passage, and he staggered helplessly. The flurry and rustle of the woman's movements made a sound like the wings of a hundred birds. The man began to protest in a weak and whining voice but the girl uttered no sound at all.

Mannering followed them, recognising the acute danger. Griselda had gone berserk, was beating and pushing the old man blindly, and he was only a few feet from the head of the stairs. If he fell, he would break his neck. But it would be useless to call out.

Mannering stepped behind Griselda, but she took no notice of his hands at her shoulders. He could feel the wiry strength of her body, muscles so taut that they seemed like sinews. The old man's eyes were closed and he was whimpering. There was a scratch, vivid red, beneath his right eye.

Mannering thrust his arms round Griselda's waist, and wrenched her away. She was so surprised that she didn't resist. He put in so much effort that, still holding her, he staggered back, her weight against him. For a moment of alarm he thought he would go crashing down on his back.

By exerting all his strength, he saved himself.

He did not save the old man, who turned round blindly and began to run, oblivious of the stairs, and as Mannering shouted: "Careful! Careful!" he went over the stairs, treading on air.

And then he crashed down.

7

MOMENT OF REMORSE

Mannering, steady now, moved forward. Griselda stood by
the side of the landing, staring down, one clenched hand at
her mouth. Mannering reached the head of the stairs as the
sound of falling stopped. He was fearful of what he might
see, and relieved when he saw the man lying on his back,
one knee pressed against the banisters which had broken
his fall.

Even from where he stood, Mannering could see that he
was breathing.

He went down the stairs, stepped over the body, then,
kneeling, tested the arms and ribs and shoulders, gently.
There was no sign of a break. The man's lips were parted
and he was breathing naturally.

The girl appeared close to the edge of the stairs.

"Is he—is he all right?"

"I think so," Mannering answered. "We ought to put him
on a couch or a bed."

"I'll turn the bed down," she said, in a flat voice; then in
a flurry of concern: "Can you manage him?"

"Oh, yes, quite easily."

She peered down for a moment, looking very young from
this angle, then disappeared. Mannering eased the man
'Ted' into his arms and carried him slowly upstairs. He was
light enough, no more than eight or nine stone. His ribs
were prominent beneath his clothes, and his face seemed all
skin and bone. His eyelids were criss-crossed with blue and

red veins, as was his nose: the sign of the regular spirit drinker.

The girl called from a doorway: "In here."

Mannering took the man into a small room with a narrow bed and a single recessed window, and put him down on spotless sheets. The girl immediately began to take off his shoes and Mannering loosened his waistband and his over-large collar. The breathing was stertorous: Mannering wondered if he had come round and was feigning. He felt the pulse and found it regular enough.

"Who is he?" he asked.

She answered with an effort: "My uncle."

"What made you lose your temper like that?"

"He'd no right to be here." When Mannering didn't answer, she went on almost desperately: "I sent him away this morning. He must have taken a key and come back while I was at work. He—" She broke off, and something like anger sparked in her eyes. "I suppose you think I'm callous."

"I know you're very upset," Mannering said gently.

"He—drives me *mad*."

"Relations can be very trying."

"He's utterly impossible. He—" She caught her breath but was soon pouring out her story in a torrent. That Ted was Edward Leo, her dead father's brother, that he was always drunk and always gambling, that he lived off her most of the year, that she didn't trust him, in fact came near to hating him. All of this came out explosively and it was obvious that she was suffering acutely from both guilt and remorse and yet was trying desperately to justify herself. "I didn't mean to push him over but there are times when I could *kill* him. He never leaves me alone, he's always spying, he's always borrowing from my friends. I tell you I hate him!"

Beyond doubt, she came very near to hate at this moment.

As obviously, Edward Leo was conscious and fully aware of what she was saying, even though he kept his eyes closed tightly. When Mannering didn't respond, the woman went on, in a tense and angry voice:

"I can't do a thing without him knowing, I can't lead a life of my own. I wish he'd broken his neck!"

"Now—" began Mannering soothingly.

"But I do. I'm sick and tired of behaving like a hypocrite. I wish he were dead! I never want to see him again. I wish—"

Suddenly, she burst into tears, and as she did so her uncle opened his eyes for a moment, only to close them again when he realised that Mannering was looking at him. Mannering did not try to comfort the girl with words, but led her into the passage and back to the big room. He helped her into the Regency chair, pushed a cushion behind her head, and then went out.

Ted was already halfway off the bed.

Mannering opened his door wide and he scrambled back.

"She could have killed me!" he cried.

"Yes," said Mannering. "Perhaps it's a pity she didn't."

"*What?*" Ted gasped, eyes rounding with well-simulated shock.

"You heard me," said Mannering. "Get up."

"But—but—but I'm hurt. I can't move!"

"Get up," Mannering ordered, "and get out." He took out his wallet, extracted two pounds and gave them to Griselda's uncle. "Don't come back. If I were you I would never come back. This time she was just angry, next time she might get really mad."

Edward Leo took the two pounds almost by sleight of hand, fastened his waistband but did not trouble to do up his shoes, or else did not know they were untied, and trotted down the beautiful staircase with a skill which told of much practice, probably when his balance wasn't very good.

Twice he disappeared only to reappear on another section of the staircase; and at last, the door slammed. Mannering did not think there was much doubt that he would head for the nearest pub and spend the money. To be sure, he had gone Mannering went down two flights of stairs. There was no sign of the old man.

Mannering went back to the big room.

Griselda was no longer crying, but was dabbing her face with a large paper handkerchief. She looked at him quite calmly, despite the puffy, red-rimmed eyes, and said in a husky voice:

"I'm sorry."

"I'd love a cup of tea," Mannering said.

"What?"

"Wouldn't you?"

"Oh," she exclaimed, and smiled faintly. "Yes, I would." She got up and spoke from the door. "I really *am* sorry I made such a fool of myself."

"We all do, at times," he dissembled. "May I look round at this furniture, while you're gone?"

"If you wish to," she said, and disappeared.

Mannering stood and looked from piece to piece, appalled by the overcrowding. He visited second-hand shops from time to time, where perhaps a single item was so abused; but, as Goodman had said, this was a treasure house, and should be kept like a museum.

As he was examining the sofa table, not finding the slightest flaw, Griselda came back to the doorway. "Mr. Mannering."

"Hallo," he exclaimed.

"They're *not* for sale," she stated.

"I wish they were," he said ruefully.

She looked at him with another change of expression, and he thought there was a touch of contempt in it; perhaps of disappointment.

"I expect you do," she said. "All men are the same. All they can think of is—" She broke off, and darted out of sight, as if afraid that she had said too much.

Mannering picked up two small vases, each a pale, translucent green. He had no doubt at all that they were Ming. He put them back, and lifted a porcelain jug with a simple Chinese design. To the uninitiated eye it would appear to have little value; yet it would fetch at least two hundred pounds at any big sale.

Why, the contents of this room were worth a fortune!

He was at the chiffonier when Griselda came back, carrying the tea on a wrought iron silver tray. The teapot was of silver, too, almost certainly early Georgian, and the cups and saucers early Doulton. She put the tray down on a Sheraton table and looked at Mannering, half-smiling, half-troubled.

"All I seem to do is say 'I'm sorry'."

"I'm having a most refreshingly different evening," Mannering remarked.

"That's one way of looking at it! I *am* sorry—that I attacked Uncle Ted, that I involved you, that I burst into tears, and was rude to you just now."

"I don't know. Perhaps men do think more in terms of money than women."

"I shouldn't have said it."

"It might be a good thing if you said what you thought, instead of bottling it up all the time," said Mannering. He watched her pour out tea; she had small but very capable-looking hands, the nails well-shaped and unpolished. "Thank you. I wasn't thinking of these lovely things in terms of money though."

"You *weren't*?"

"No."

"Then what were you thinking?"

"That they're wasted here."

"Well!" she exclaimed. "You believe in speaking your mind, don't you?"

"At times. Every piece here is a gem."

"Do you think I don't realise that?" she demanded.

"If you realise it, why do you hide them away from everybody?" asked Mannering.

She went very, very pale.

He had then, for the first time, an inkling of what was wrong. It was no more than an inkling, a dawning of understanding, but it was also a warning of what might come and it made him both more sympathetic and yet wary of her. Her eyes had a curiously cold and lifeless expression: as if she had been hurt so much but was resisting hurt now. The phrase which had stabbed at her was 'why do you hide them away from everybody', and that told him that she was indeed hiding them.

He could drop the subject, but if he did it would cause constraint between them and he would not be able to talk freely, nor would he be likely to get any information from her. There was nearly as much danger if he kept probing, but that seemed to him the right thing to do; she would probably respond to honesty.

"Well, why?" he asked.

"What I do is no business of yours," she said stiffly.

"I might be able to help," he stated.

"I don't need your help."

"Don't you?" asked Mannering, and after a pause, asked a question as if idly: "Do you think it wiser to lie to yourself, or to someone else?"

She muttered: "I'm not lying."

"Yes you are," Mannering retorted very gently. "You need help very much, and for some reason you're frightened of getting it. I don't believe that pride would stand in your way."

She was silent for a long time, before she said stiffly:

"Mr. Mannering, I asked you to come and see some jewels. Will you examine them, please? I can pay your fee for valuation if it's reasonable."

"I would like to see them very much," he assured her.

She put her cup down, got up and went to the corner cupboard. She took a key from a pocket in her dress, and opened the right-hand door. First she drew out a small portable typewriter, then a small, flat square box. She pushed the cupboard door to and brought the box to Mannering, placing it in front of him.

"Please open it."

Slowly, he opened the box.

Although velvet-lined, in a deep green, this was not the original case for the jewellery; the rings, the necklace and the earrings were all a little too large, and had been pressed into the spaces too tightly, so that he had to prise them free with the handle of a spoon. He took out first the larger of two rings, then the bracelet, next one of the brooches. He placed these on the polished table and then, slipping a magnifying glass from his pocket, peered at them intently.

He was as sure as he could be without making further tests, that the diamonds and the emeralds were genuine. He examined the settings; they were of gold, and the work of a seventeenth-century French jewelsmith. He put the pieces back in their spaces, but did not touch the others.

"Aren't you going to look at the others?" Griselda asked, quite sharply.

"Not now."

"Why not?"

"These are enough to convince me that they're real," he replied.

She drew a deep breath, as if in relief, and her expression softened for the first time.

"So they *are* real, then."

"Of course. Didn't you know they were?"

"I couldn't be sure," she muttered.

"Any expert would have told you."

Her eyes seemed to grow larger and larger, and this time there was no doubt at all of her breathtaking truthfulness, when she said:

"I couldn't consult experts."

"Why not?"

"Because they might have come to the conclusion that these were stolen. And if they had they might have brought the police here."

Having said that, she held her breath.

Mannering pushed the box of jewels aside, finished his first cup of tea, and then handed the empty cup to her.

"May I have some more? ... Thank you ... And *are* they stolen?"

Her eyes looked positively huge and there was deep appeal in them as she answered:

"Yes."

"Are you sure?" asked Mannering.

"Yes."

"Do you know who stole them?"

"Yes."

"Who?"

"My father," she stated simply.

There was no doubt at all in her mind, and she convinced Mannering absolutely. He had not expected such devastating honesty but he managed to conceal most of his surprise as he asked:

"Is your father alive?"

"No."

"Your mother?"

"My only living relative is Uncle Edward," she said, "and you know how devoted I am to him." She drew a deep breath, and narrowed her eyes, as if pain had suddenly stabbed at her. "Mr. Mannering," she went on.

"Yes?"

"Would you lend me some money on the security of these jewels?" When he didn't answer immediately, she went on with a touch of desperation: "A lot of money, I mean. I need five thousand pounds."

The jewels which lay between them were worth fifty thousand pounds, if not more. There was no way of telling whether this girl knew that, and it was not the immediate issue. That was, whether to say 'no', because it was—or at least should be—impossible to accept stolen jewels as security, or whether to ask further questions in the hope that he would learn more from her if she thought there was a possibility that he would advance the money.

Her eyes seemed to burn; her whole body seemed to plead. But she had been astonishingly honest with him and he did not see how he could be anything less than honest with her. So, hating the hurt and disappointment he knew were inevitable for her, he said:

"No, Griselda. I won't lend you money against jewels I believe to have been stolen. That would only be compounding the felony and in the long run wouldn't help either you or me."

He did not know what to expect. Tears would not have surprised him, or an outburst of anger, her nerves were so much on edge. What he didn't expect was the light touch of her fingers on the back of his hand, and the smile as she breathed:

"Thank God, I seem to have found an *honest* man."

8

HONEST MAN

Griselda looked delighted. The transformation in her face was quite remarkable and Mannering was suddenly aware of the beauty that could be in her; how radiant her eyes could be and how shapely her lips were beneath the daubed-on lipstick. He was taken aback enough to give a little laugh, and to say:

"They're about in droves!"

"Honest men?" she asked, and the radiance died. "They're harder to find than a swallow in winter."

What had so disillusioned her? What would make her so sweeping in her condemnation? This was no time to ask; there were so many other things he wanted to know. He was momentarily afraid that 'they're about in droves' would have made her broody again, but she seemed lighter-hearted than before.

"Well," Mannering said, "let's assume I am honest. Where does that take us?"

She said: "I need the help of an honest man who knows about antiques and precious stones. All these things," she added, and waved her hand almost casually about the room. "I did inherit them, as I told you in my letter. My father left them to me with this house." She half-closed her eyes and her voice seemed to fade. "We were so happy when he was at home. So happy. I can remember—" She broke off abruptly and opened her eyes wide, as if with great effort. "But you don't want to hear about what it used to be like here!"

"Have you lived here all your life?" Mannering asked.

"I came here when I was six," she told him.

"With your parents?"

"Yes," she answered, and pain crossed her face again. "Yes, just for a few years. Daddy came out of prison, and we went to Australia, but after a few years we came back and he bought this house. It was—beautiful. I still don't know much about antiques, but I loved everything in the house. If it comes to that," she added, looking at him with defiant candour, "I still do."

"I can tell you do," murmured Mannering.

"You do, in a way, don't you?" she said. "Tell me, Mr. Mannering—do you love these things because of what they look like, or because they are old, or—or even because they are so terribly scarce and fetch such a lot of money?"

"A little of the first two," he said. "And something else, I think."

"What something else?" she demanded.

"Because they're more than works of art: they're works of love," Mannering answered. "And some are a part of Britain. Craftsmen made them, often craftsmen who came from a long line of craftsmen. Did you ever pause to think that crafts can be handed down through generations, but creative art comes out only when it will?"

She was frowning slightly as he went on:

"It's a fact. As for the money side of it: buying and selling and valuing is my trade. I like the profit I make. I wouldn't if I made too much."

"That's what I mean," said Griselda. "You're an honest man. Mr. Mannering, I've a terrible problem."

"Tell me," he urged gently.

"Thank you," she said simply. "Thank you for asking me to. Well, I didn't know until about eight years ago, just after my father died, that everything here was stolen. Even the house was bought with stolen money. My mother told me, only a few days before she died." Griselda closed her eyes tightly, as if to shut out some vision. "They were both killed in a car crash. Daddy died instantaneously but Mummy lived for nearly a week. She didn't tell me the truth until she knew she was dying."

"I see," said Mannering. He did not know what to say or how to help this girl. There had been occasions when he had been told such a story and he had wondered how much was true, but it did not occur to him to doubt the truth of what Griselda was telling him. He guessed she had not told him everything, but hoped that with patience he would hear more.

"Are you alone, now?"

"Except for Uncle Edward," she said bitterly.

"Did he come here when your parents were alive?"

"Daddy wouldn't have him near the house," she answered. "He gave him a kind of pension, five hundred pounds a year, and met him in London now and again. It wasn't until I was here on my own that he came. He—" She shut her eyes again, helplessly. "He offered to be the man of the house, to look after me. He did stay for a few months but he was so drunk most of the time even I couldn't stand it. Then he won some money gambling and went away for a while, but he always comes back." At last, she opened her eyes. "He's just a parasite," she stated flatly. "He hasn't done an honest day's work in his life. Parasite is the only word for him."

"But whenever he's come, you've let him stay," Mannering remarked gently.

"Well," she said wearily. "I had to."

"How do you mean, had to?"

"He *is* my uncle," she said, and then in a stronger voice, went on: "Besides, I was frightened in case he told the police about the furniture and all these things. Being stolen, I mean." Again she paused, and then she squared her shoulders and went on. "So I wasn't exactly filled with brotherly love. I was afraid he would tell everyone who I was, and—and I hated the prospect. Partly for myself," she added candidly, "but mostly because I hated the thought of Daddy's memory—" She broke off again and tears shimmered in her eyes. In a funny kind of voice and pulling a funny kind of face, she went on. "We human beings are the victims of circumstances, aren't we? We haven't really got free will. We have to do what our own emotions, our fears and hopes and circumstances push us into doing. We're *always* being pushed."

"We surely have the free will to resist," Mannering argued mildly.

"That's *almost* sanctimonious," she retorted.

"You're almost sick with self-pity," Mannering replied, in a tone so gentle that it almost concealed the sharpness of the reproof. But not quite. Her eyes widened in momentary resentment, and then she raised her hands to a level with her breast and let them fall into her lap.

"I suppose I am," she admitted. "I *do* pity myself."

"You'll go on pitying yourself unless you stop hating everybody," Mannering replied.

She gasped.

"You have got a nerve!"

"Griselda Leo," Mannering said flatly, "what do you want from me? Easy reassurances, and 'there-there—never mind'?"

After a while, and smiling faintly, she answered. "No. Can you guess what I want from you?" Now, she was challenging.

"Yes," Mannering said. "The impossible."

"*What?*"

"You want me to find a way to enable you to cash in on all these things, stolen or not, without getting into trouble with the police, and without troubling your conscience. On what you've told me so far, it's impossible. But is that generally true, though?"

"What you really mean," said Griselda in a sharper voice than she had yet used, "is that you're not impressed by my hard luck story, and won't help."

Mannering put his head on one side, and pursed his lips. There was a glint of amusement in his eyes, and an answering one in hers. He liked this girl. Now that she felt at ease with him, much of her true quality was showing.

"No," he said. "Do you want to sell your treasures?"

"No," she answered. "I want to borrow against them."

"I'm not a money-lender, Griselda."

"Do you mean you would buy them but not lend money?" she flashed.

"Not on the jewels," Mannering said.

"Why not?"

"They are still on the records at Scotland Yard as stolen."

"Oh," she said, and paled. "Oh." She seemed to shrivel up, but still faced him boldly. "Do the police know I have them?"

"Not from me, at all events."

"Did you check when you had my letter?"

"Yes," said Mannering.

"I see." She shifted in her chair, and as she did so a door banged somewhere in the passage.

"That's my bedroom door," she said. "I left the window open." She stood up and moved about, running her fingers over the precious pieces round the room; and he could not see the slightest sign of dust, she kept everything here as if she loved it. "So, it's no use."

"Why do you want five thousand pounds?" Mannering asked, and almost as if it were a reflex action, she answered.

"To repay a debt."

For the first time, he didn't believe her. The glibness of the reply together with some slight change in her expression, a kind of wariness, warned him of this. He let it pass; there would be another time to challenge her.

"It must be a big debt," he remarked.

She said, a little too quickly. "I went into a business, and lost it. My partner—my partner went ill, and I couldn't carry on by myself." When Mannering made no comment Griselda went on with a note of near-desperation: "It was a bookshop. I work in a bookshop now."

"Will five thousand pounds clear all your debts?" Mannering asked, and her eyes went suddenly bright.

"Oh, yes!"

"Will you give me a lien on any pieces of furniture here that I select, against a loan of five thousand pounds?" asked Mannering quietly.

He knew that the furniture round these walls was worth at least fifty thousand, but she might not. He knew that she loved this furniture but he did not know whether her need of the money was desperate enough to make her use it and the *objets* as security. At first, she sat there, very pale, biting her lips. He saw her hands trembling as she held them in front of her in that characteristic pose. She gave a little shiver that ran through her whole body.

"Will you—will you do that?"

"On one condition," Mannering said.

"What condition?" She moved so that she could lean against the back of one of the Chippendale chairs, and she was still trembling all over.

"That it stays here."

"Oh, good God!" she exclaimed. "Where else would it be? Supposing—supposing the police find out?" She was whispering, as if she could not really believe that his offer was serious.

"I doubt if any of this furniture could be identified as

stolen," Mannering said. "In any case, it would be my risk. Yours would be that you might lose your antiques if you couldn't repay the money."

With a faint smile, as if she were recovering from the shock, she said:

"That would be *my* risk."

"Yes indeed," Mannering said drily. "Do you know how long it will take you to repay the loan?"

"At least—at least a year," she answered.

"Five thousand pounds at seven per cent for twelve months—is that it?"

"Oh, good God!" she exclaimed again. *"Please."*

Slowly, he put his hand to his inside breast pocket, and drew out his cheque book. A dozen questions were flashing through his mind; why did she really want the money? Was there the slightest chance of her paying it back; was she under any kind of pressure—being blackmailed, for instance?

"Do you take dictation?" he asked.

"Yes." She glanced round at the portable typewriter.

"Then supposing we have a letter in duplicate which we each sign, as a form of agreement," he suggested.

She turned round and pulled out a drawer of the sofa table, took out a notebook, and breathed:

"Yes."

"Then I'll dictate: 'Dear Miss Leo. This is to confirm my offer of a loan of five thousand pounds payable today and repayable within the next twelve months at an annual interest rate of seven per cent against the security of the following pieces of furniture, twelve in all'." She was taking the dictation very quickly. "'One: a set of four chairs by Chippendale, a French sofa table, a walnut cabinet, *circa* 1725, by Rotes...'"

When at last he finished, she said in obvious admiration: "You've hardly looked at them!"

"I have learned to back my own judgment," Mannering countered. "If you'll do the letter I'll write the cheque."

Her typing speed was as good as her shorthand speed, and, the cheque signed, Mannering watched her. She had much grace of movement, arms moving only to shift the carriage, fingers glowing with light touch and, presumably, absolute accuracy. She pulled the letter out of the machine and handed him the top copy and read the carbon itself. There was no error.

"That's perfectly all right," Mannering said. "Shall we sign?"

Each signed, and now Griselda's hands were trembling. He handed her his copy, and the cheque. She stared at it for a few seconds, and then dropped back into the chair, obviously fighting back tears.

The door outside banged again.

"I *must* get that door fixed," she said in vexed tones, but she sat without moving. "I—I can't possibly tell you—" She broke off. "It's unbelievable!" she choked. "When I wrote to you I hoped, but I didn't really think. It's—it's as if a great weight's gone." Tears began to spill down her cheeks. "Oh, I know I'm being silly, but it's such a relief, such a tremendous relief." She sat there, the tears streaming down her cheeks, in strange silence.

As they sat, Mannering heard a footfall in the passage.

He turned very swiftly, and put his fingers to his lips as he strode across the room. It was probably Uncle Ted listening at the keyhole, he seemed able to get in and out at will. Mannering gripped the handle of the door firmly, and pulled.

The door did not open.

He pulled again with more strength, but it still did not budge. She sprang up to join him and Mannering heard more footsteps, less stealthy, in the passage or on the stairs. He pulled with all his strength but now felt sure that the key had been turned in the lock outside. He dropped to one knee, taking out a penknife which had a picklock blade, but even if he could get the lock turned quickly there was little chance of catching the intruder.

"Who could have done it," Griselda gasped, and then said in a tone of bitter realisation: "Ted!"

The lock clicked back.

Mannering pulled the door open and rushed out. There were footsteps at the bottom of the stairs, heavy and urgent now—heavier than those of Griselda's uncle were likely to be. He reached the first carved banister and peered down the well.

He caught a glimpse of a man whom he could not possibly mistake but whose presence here was utterly unbelievable: of Black Knight, glancing upwards before he sprang out of sight.

The downstairs door slammed.

9

DISASTER

There was just a chance of catching the man.

Mannering turned to Griselda and cried: "Wait here!" and began to run downstairs. He must be careful, they were narrow and quite steep and tapered away to an inch close to the wall at the curves. He reached the first landing, and then caught sight of a piece of rusty metal, a doorstop, two or three treads down at the next flight. He grabbed the handrail and checked himself, stopping at the obstruction. Because of the curve he could not have cleared it with a jump, he must have crashed down. He stepped over carefully and ran on, but now he had no hope at all.

He pulled open the door as a car engine roared, just beyond the wall. He caught a glimpse of the blue top of a car going away from Farnham. With luck he would be able to see the number and identify the make. He nearly slipped on a clump of grass, slowed down and reached the gate. Several cars were coming towards him, heading for Farnham proper, but only one, an old-fashioned blue Vauxhall, was going away from him. He couldn't see the number but the Aston Martin had a turn of speed that would soon catch the other car up. He wrenched open the door, slid beneath the driving wheel, and pulled the self-starter.

There was a sharp explosion. Smoke and flame billowed out from beneath the bonnet followed by a rattle of metal, but nothing struck the windscreen. Two long-legged girls on the other side of the road turned their heads, a motorist jammed on his brakes, while the flames and the smoke grew thicker and fiercer. Mannering, calm now the crisis was upon him, unhitched the fire-extinguisher from the door panel and got out, almost choked by the smoke.

At any moment there might be another explosion.

He pressed the knob of the fire extinguisher, sending foam between the bonnet and the chassis, while a young man from the passing car which had stopped, pulled on a thick glove, made no bones about the danger, and thrust the bonnet up. More flames leapt. Mannering sprayed the whole of the engine while the young man produced another extinguisher and sprayed as calmly. By then, a dozen people had gathered at a safe distance, including the two girls. The flames receded quickly, leaving the engine and the side of the car a foamy, smelly mess. There was no smoke now.

"Well," said Mannering to the young man, "I'll never be able to thank you."

"No need," the other replied, smiling quite happily. "I'm always glad to test my reflexes. They weren't bad, were they?" he added almost smugly. "Lovely job you've got, sir."

"It won't get me far tonight," said Mannering ruefully.

"What happened?" asked the young man.

If Mannering told him the simple truth the story would be all over Farnham very quickly and almost certainly the London newspapers would take it up. He didn't want that, yet; didn't want it generally known that Black Knight was really seeking revenge. And he did not want Griselda Leo involved in any sensation or she would be harassed by the Press, a bad thing at this moment.

So he said: "That's what I have to find out." He looked up at the crowd. "Did anybody see what happened?"

Nobody admitted having seen a thing.

The two long-legged girls, in their early teens, had been

startled by the explosion but noticed nothing before that.

"I'd better get the wreckage towed to a garage," Mannering said, heavily.

"I'm going to fill up with petrol at my garage," said the helpful young man who was tall, lean and very clean-cut. "They've a breakdown van. Shall I have them send it?"

"Please," said Mannering gratefully.

He did not know how to get rid of the crowd which was growing larger every moment. He half-expected Griselda to come out but there was no sign of her. Then a police car drew up and two uniformed men got out and came towards him. One was tall and thin, the other as tall but thick-set and heavy.

"Trouble, sir?" the thin one asked.

"My car caught fire," Mannering said.

"Hallo, Jim," said the clean-cut and helpful young man. "I'm going to ask Smithy's to look after it."

"All right, Micky. Have you taken any details?"

"Not being on duty, no."

The other policeman was ushering the crowd out of the road. The thin officer took details of Mannering's name and address, showing not the slightest sign of recognition. The crowd melted away. The helpful young off-duty policeman with the great presence of mind drove off and within ten minutes a breakdown van arrived. The driver, who looked no more than an oil-stained urchin with curly hair and the face of an angel, asked:

"Like me to send a taxi, sir?"

"Good idea," said Mannering. "In half-an-hour, say."

With a welcome sense that everything was perfectly under control, he went back to the house. The calmness of the police impressed him, for they must suspect that there was more to this than he had yet said. The fact that Griselda hadn't come out puzzled him, unless it was simply that she was shy of crowds—or possibly feared an encounter with a policeman. The door marked 47d was closed, which puzzled him even more.

He rang the bell.

It seemed a long time before there was any movement inside, much longer than the first time he had rung. Some-one nearby was using a motor-mower; and somewhere a child was crying. Bees hummed about the old red rambler and among the flowers in the grass.

At last the door opened.

Griselda looked as if she were about to faint. She held onto the door and gazed at Mannering, her mouth slack. There was no doubt at all, she was in shock; it was a marvel that she had got down the stairs at all. He took her arm, closed the door, and said quietly:

"Just relax, Griselda. Try to relax."

He put an arm beneath her knees and the other beneath her shoulders and lifted her. By leaning against the wall, at the curves, he was able to get up without difficulty, but she wasn't a light weight, nearer nine than eight stone, he guessed. He was breathing heavily when he reached the top of the stairs. As he lowered her to the ground he noticed her eyes. Both shock and fear were in her expression.

"What is it?" he asked gently.

She said: "Ted."

"Uncle Ted?"

She nodded, but did not try to speak again.

He looked along the passage and saw that the door of the little room was open. There was a slight breeze, and he remembered the slamming of the doors. He pushed past her and reached the open door and looked inside.

There was Griselda's Uncle Ted, who must have sneaked back.

Someone had smashed in the front of his head.

. . . . .

Mannering did not need to check the pulse: beyond all doubt the old man was dead. And here was Griselda, who had said that she hated him and who had wished him dead, in shock. He himself was shocked, too, all sense that things were orderly had gone.

Could *she* have killed the man?

Nonsense! Black Knight had been here.

Much more likely the shock was the result of her coming to this door and seeing what he saw.

He turned back, leaving everything untouched. Somehow the picture of the blood-spattered pillow and the blood-spattered wall was more vivid and more ugly in his memory than it had been in reality. He repressed a shiver as he put his arm about the girl and led her into the big room.

There, on the floor, was his cheque for five thousand pounds; and, on the sofa table, the two signed letters.

"Sit down, Griselda," he said, and when she lowered herself slowly to a chair, he went on: "What happened?"

She simply said: "Ted."

"Yes, I know."

"I—I found him," she said.

He was torn by the fact that the police must soon be told and by the compulsive desire to help the girl. A wild thought, that he might take her away, flashed in and out of his mind. She needed a doctor, and a sedative: treatment for shock. It would be folly to delay that long. There was only one good thing: she was in no shape to answer questions, the moment a doctor saw her that would be established. So, he needed a doctor first.

Griselda sat, staring in front of her, blankly.

"Is there a telephone?" he asked.

She didn't speak.

"Griselda, have you a telephone?"

Still she didn't answer.

If there were an instrument up here he would have

noticed it; he must go and find a telephone. There might be one in a downstairs flat. He hated to leave her alone, but it would be better than taking her with him.

Or—would it?

The taxi should soon be here.

He knew that if he took her away without reporting what had happened he would be asking for trouble with the police, trouble for her, as well as trouble for himself. He had never been in a predicament where it was more difficult to decide what to do. But before long, he concluded that whatever the risk he must get her to a doctor.

There was a ring at a bell somewhere in the flat—the front door bell, presumably. Police? He moved away from Griselda, not needing to warn her to stay where she was, and hurried down the stairs, thinking: I need someone else to look after her. He picked up the doorstop, over which he had so nearly fallen—and there was something sticky on it.

God! he thought: that's blood.

His heart seemed to turn over.

He placed the doorstop at the foot of the stairs, close to the wall, and looked at his right hand; the palm and inside of the fingers were smeared with blood.

He opened the door with his left hand, to a short, paunchy man with tired eyes and a sad face, who touched the peak of his chauffeur's hat, and said:

"You want a cab, sir?"

Mannering gulped.

"Yes. I also need to make a telephone call, urgently."

"There's a phone downstairs here," the man told him, brightly.

"Good! And—do you know Mr. Goodman, the antique dealer?"

"Who doesn't," the taxi driver answered.

"Will you go and ask him if he can come and see me—John Mannering—at once? Tell him it's an emergency."

"An emergency," the taxi driver repeated, and then to Mannering's surprise he gave a broad smile, and said: "Getting a lot of them today, aren't you? Okay, I'll tell him. Will you tell *me* something?"

"If I can," promised Mannering.

"How long will you want my cab? I've got three jobs tonight, if you're going to want me for more than an hour I'd better get someone else to take the others."

"I'd like you for the rest of the evening," Mannering said. He moved his hand towards his pocket, to take out his wallet, but stopped. The wallet would be all smeared with blood, so would any money he touched. "I'll see you all right," he promised.

"Okay," said the taxi driver. "It's a deal."

Mannering left the door on the latch, and turned round, scrutinising the doorstop without again touching it. It was undoubtedly the murder weapon. It had been near the top of the stairs when he had arrived and had avoided tripping over it. The murder committed, it must have been brought back to its original position near the door. Mannering wiped his hand as clean as he could, and walked round the house to the front porch. The white paint on the door was flaking and dirty. As it opened, a burly man stood there with two small children clinging to his knees. They stared up.

"Yes?" the man asked gruffly.

"I need to get a doctor for Miss Leo," Mannering said. "She's been taken ill. Do you have a telephone I can use?"

"In the hall, help yourself," the man replied. He had broad features and a broken nose, full lips and one cauliflower ear. "Is it serious?"

"She certainly needs a doctor," Mannering repeated.

"She alone?"

"Yes."

"I'll phone," said the man. "She want a woman's help?

My wife'll go up like a shot."

"If she needs a woman I'll let you know at once," Mannering promised. "You're very good."

"Ta," cooed one of the children.

"Man," remarked the other as if in great discovery.

Mannering had the presence of mind to smile down at them before he left. He felt both tension and relief as he went up the stairs. At the top, the narrow passage seemed to go round, the whole house went round and round. He grabbed the banister rail and felt himself toppling backwards, held on with all his strength, and then slowly recovered from the attack of giddiness.

He moved slowly towards the room in which he had left Griselda. She looked up at him vaguely, then down again.

The cheque was still on the floor; the letter was still there. He picked up the cheque, and then noticed that the jewels were no longer on the table. His heart seemed to turn over. The box was there but all the jewels were gone. He glanced about him but saw no sign of them.

"Griselda!" he exclaimed. "The jewels, where are the jewels?"

She looked at him blankly.

He spun round to the corner cupboard, the door of which was still open; nothing was inside. He opened every drawer in sight, but there were no jewels, nothing of value. He looked under the table, and then turned to Griselda again, and said in a low-pitched voice:

"Griselda. Where are the jewels?"

There was only dullness in her eyes, and when her lips moved, all she said, and that almost inaudibly, was: "Ted."

As the whispered name wavered about the room, there was a ring at the front door bell.

10

MISSING JEWELS

Mannering moved slowly away from the girl and reached the passage as the bell rang again, a longer ring this time, hinting at impatience. As he reached the top of the stairs a current of wind swept up; and close by, a door banged. It reminded him of Griselda, telling him the wind kept banging her door.

"Are you there?" It was Frank Goodman from the bottom of the stairs.

"Yes. Come up," called Mannering.

Goodman came running up, nimble as a boy and youthful-looking despite the beard. His eyes were bright and eager.

"Is everything all right, Mr. Mannering?"

"On the contrary, everything is all wrong," Mannering said gruffly.

"You mean—Miss Leo?"

"Mr. Goodman," Mannering said, "she has had a very great shock. I have to go to the police at once, and I don't want to leave her alone. A doctor has been sent for by the tenant of the downstairs flat but I don't know how long he'll be. I wanted someone here who could keep his head.

They stood close together on the landing, Goodman breathing as evenly as if he hadn't run up at least thirty-six steps. He paused for a few moments, taking in all Mannering said, and then he asked:

"What kind of shock did she have?"

"Her uncle has been murdered."

"*Murdered?*" Goodman echoed.

Mannering said: "His body is in a room along there."

Goodman looked beyond him towards the open door. A shadow moved, of a tree against the passage wall. Suddenly, Goodman brushed his hand across his forehead, and said:

"That's a hell of a thing to happen. The very idea makes me feel sick." And after a moment he added: "I can't imagine what it's done for Griselda."

That was the first time Mannering had heard him use Griselda's Christian name. He liked Goodman's reaction, even the fact that he was so obviously shaken; and he liked it when the other asked:

"Where is she?"

"In her room. Will you stay with her?"

"Yes," said Goodman simply. "Be glad to."

He did not ask why Mannering had sent for him, but braced himself and went into the room just behind Mannering. He did not look about him, but walked straight to Griselda, who was now sitting upright in her chair, hands in her lap. Her hair had become dishevelled and was no longer drawn tightly back from her forehead. It had a softening effect, spoiled by her expression of utter hopelessness.

"Griselda," Mannering said. "I'm going out. Mr. Goodman will stay here until I get back."

She did not speak, or nod, or show any sign that she had heard and understood. Goodman put a hand on her shouldder, as natural as could be.

Mannering didn't speak again, but went out.

There was the murdered man; there was the shocked girl; there was Black Knight and the explosion in the car; and now, in a way the most crushing blow of all, there was the disappearance of the diamonds. Obviously it was possible that someone had been hiding in the flat and stolen them when he had gone chasing after Knight, although there had been no sign of anyone. And it was just as possible that the girl had taken them: that she was acting a part for some reason he could not begin to guess.

He actually shook his head.

"I don't believe it," he said aloud.

He glanced at the doorstop as he went down the last flight of stairs, but did not touch it. He went out, to find the taxi driver in the gateway, talking to the burly neighbour, who now had one child perched on his shoulder and the other cradled in his left arm.

The burly man was speaking, but broke off as Mannering drew up.

"I was just saying, there's something bloody funny going on here."

"Have you spoken to the doctor?" asked Mannering.

"Dr. Pollinger is on the way," the burly man replied. "What *is* going on, that's what I want to know." There was something aggressive in his manner, and he looked capable of trying to force an answer.

The child on his shoulder said: "Man."

The child in his arm beamed and stretched a hand towards Mannering, and said: "Ta."

"The police will soon be here, you must ask them," Mannering temporised. "And thank you for your help." He turned to the taxi driver. "Take me to the police station, will you?" He waved to the children, giving each a bright smile, and went outside the garden to the waiting taxi.

His own car had gone.

There remained a patch of badly scorched grass and a section of smoke-blackened wall. No one was in sight. Mannering got into the back of the taxi, a big, black Humber, the taxi driver closed the door and took the wheel. Mannering leaned back and closed his eyes. He had mental pictures of the jewels, all eight pieces, all so rare and lovely; and he had pictures of Ted's head and his own bloodstained hand.

They reached the bottom of the Borough, and turned right.

"Mister," the driver said.

The last thing Mannering wanted to make him do was talk, but he had been prompt and very helpful.

"Yes?" Mannering asked.

"Going to stop by for a pick-me-up before you see the police?"

Mannering was startled. "No, thanks." It dawned on him that he was both hungry and thirsty, and that a meal or even a snack would do him a lot of good. Then he found himself surprised into a laugh. "Do I look as if I need a drink?"

"Look as if you've seen a ghost," the driver said. "You okay?"

"Yes, thanks."

"Can tell you something," offered the taxi driver.

"Can you?"

"The man you want is Chief Inspector Cooper. Don't be put off with anyone else. He's on duty tonight, I happen to know. We cabbies get to know a lot of things," he added, not smugly but in a most matter-of-fact way.

"You're very good," Mannering replied.

Before long they pulled into the forecourt of a modern building, where half-a-dozen police cars stood about. One moved off as they drew up, and two policemen hurried out of the building, staring at Mannering.

"Will you do something for me?" Mannering asked, taking out his card. "Telephone this number and tell my wife, who will answer, that I've been delayed and I'm not sure when I'll be back."

"Okay," promised the taxi driver, getting out and opening Mannering's door. Then he gave a huge grin and an enormous wink. "But they won't keep you in, not a gentleman like you. Don't forget: *Cooper.*"

.   /   .   .   .

Chief Inspector Cooper was a younger man than Mannering had expected; probably in his late thirties. He was dressed in a grey suit of conventional cut, and wore a pale grey tie: a tie that seemed to match his eyes. His desk was set slantwise across a square-shaped room which had two long windows, one of them overlooking trees. The uniformed constable who had brought Mannering up from the desk went out of the room but left the door open and stayed in the passage, almost as if he were on guard.

Cooper motioned to a chair.

"Good evening, Mr. Mannering. I'd heard you were in Farnham, and I'm not too surprised at your calling."

"Really?" Mannering said. He was conscious of his appearance: he must look all-in if the taxi driver had been so impressed. "Why?"

"The little explosion wasn't exactly an accident," stated Cooper.

"No," admitted Mannering. "No. How did you find out?"

"There were traces of nitroglycerine in very small quantities. Who wants to kill you, Mr. Mannering?"

"I took it more as a warning," said Mannering, and then he recalled Black Knight's visit to the shop, and his threat, and he threw up his hands. "Probably I'm wrong. A lot of people hate me for having helped to send them to prison."

"Ah," Cooper said. "It's a policeman's lot to accept such a consequence, but when a private individual takes a hand—" He broke off. "Do you know who this was, Mr. Mannering?"

Mannering hesitated, and then said slowly: "I must be absolutely sure before I name anyone."

"Of course," said Cooper. and he added drily: "Mind you, that won't help you much if the man tries again and pulls it off."

Mannering stared for a moment, made no comment, and then asked evenly: "No. Chief Inspector, is your canteen still open?"

"Canteen? Of course." Cooper was immediately anxious to please. "You look a bit bushed, I must say. Would you like a drink, or—"

"Can I settle for coffee and sandwiches?"

"That's easy. Simms!" The man outside came in. "Nip up to the canteen for coffee and sandwiches for Mr. Mannering." He sounded very much the man in authority and the man Simms went off almost at the double. "That will soon be here," promised Cooper.

"You're very kind," said Mannering. "I hope you'll feel as charitable when I've told you what I really came to see you about."

"Oh. Been keeping something up your sleeve?" Cooper smiled, as if to establish a mood of imperturbability, but his eyes were wary. "What is it?"

Mannering said: "Do you know a man named Ted Leo?"

"I know of him," said Cooper. "He's Griselda Leo's uncle."

"He was," said Mannering.

His head was aching almost intolerably and he wasn't sure he was doing a good job, but he saw the gradual hardening in the policeman's expression, and had to hand it to Cooper: apart from that, he showed no sign of being shocked.

"You mean he is dead?"

"Yes. Murdered."

Now, Cooper moved his right hand towards a telephone, but did not touch it as he said:

"Where?"

"In Griselda Leo's flat."

"When?"

"When I got back after the car trouble, she was in a

state of shock. Her uncle had been struck over the head, I think with an iron doorstop which had previously been put on the stairs to trip me up. I moved it." Mannering held out his right hand where there were streaks and smears of dried blood, brown in colour now that it had coagulated.

"Why didn't you send for us at once?" Cooper said, and flicked down a switch and spoke into a microphone on the box. "Is Inspector Mulley there?"

A man said: "I'm here, sir."

"We need a murder team, at once," said Cooper, without shifting his gaze from Mannering. "How long will you be?"

The man said: "Ten minutes, sir."

"Not a moment longer. And send four men up to 47 The Borough and station one at each of the doors. Better have a car outside, too."

"Right, sir."

Cooper flicked off, and settled back in his chair. The set of his square chin created a hard expression: he was probably as good as his own obvious opinion of himself. In a way it was a relief that the taxi driver had recommended him so readily.

"Well?"

"I had to send for a doctor for the girl. I had to get someone to stay with her. And I wasn't exactly on top form," said Mannering.

"That I can imagine," Cooper conceded. "But we could have sent for a doctor—we need the police surgeon, anyway."

"No doubt," said Mannering.

"What are you implying?" Cooper was obviously exerting himself to be very matter-of-fact.

"I thought she should have a doctor who was independent of the police," Mannering said. "She seemed very much alone."

"She is," agreed Cooper. "Who is staying with her?"

"A man named Frank Goodman, whom I'd met in the afternoon and who seemed well-disposed towards her."

"Frank Goodman?" repeated Cooper.

"Yes."

Cooper said: "How long is it since you found the body?"

"Griselda Leo found the body," Mannering corrected. "From the time I saw it, I suppose thirty minutes. Perhaps forty."

As he answered Police Constable Simms came in with a tray, laden with coffee, some thick and appetising-looking sandwiches and some biscuits and cheese. He placed this on a corner of Cooper's desk and stood back sharply.

"Everything all right, sir?"

"Yes." Cooper turned to Mannering. "Let me take some scrapings of that blood, then Simms will show you where to wash your hands."

Mannering obeyed, then followed the man gratefully. Returning cleaned and refreshed, he found an added zest as he reached for a sandwich. It probably wasn't surprising to Cooper that he could eat and drink quite normally. The police were used to death; he, himself, was not. He had come upon death by violence often enough but would never really get used to it. Yet despite this he ate and drank with relish, while Cooper took some papers on his desk and appeared intent on them. He certainly had himself under strict control.

He looked up.

"How well do you know Griselda Leo?"

"I'd never met her until tonight."

"Why did you come to Farnham?"

"She asked me to do some valuations," Mannering said, half-truthfully.

"Of what?"

"Jewels and furniture."

"And did you?"

Mannering said: "I agreed to lend her five thousand pounds against twelve antique pieces in her room which were worth at least ten times as much, but I did no close valuation. While we were talking . . ."

He told the story of the banging door, the man he had glimpsed, and his chase, but he still did not mention Knight. There was a whole area of enquiries he wanted to make and at this stage he did not want to tell the police anything more than they could easily find out. He did not know whether Cooper suspected this, and had a feeling that the policeman was also being reticent. He finished a third sandwich and his first cup of coffee when the box on the desk buzzed.

Cooper switched on: "Yes?"

"All ready to go," reported Mulley.

"Then go. I'll be along when I can. Send for me if you think it's urgent."

"Right, sir." Mulley and Cooper switched off at almost the identical moment and the box gave a little resonant twang.

Cooper pursed his lips before giving a faint smile.

"If you had your way, where would you be now, Mr. Mannering?" he asked.

"In London," Mannering answered promptly.

"You mean you're not aching to get to the scene of the crime?"

"No," Mannering said feelingly. "I am not. The girl should be all right, and there certainly isn't anything I can do at the house." He poured himself another cup of coffee, and sat back. "The question is, where do you think I should be?"

There was a long silence; a silence which Cooper deliberately prolonged. But at last he answered: "I think I should hold you here, for questioning—what they euphemistically call 'helping the police with their enquiries'. You don't seriously think that I can let you go, Mr. Mannering, do you?"

11

ULTIMATUM

Mannering went very still.

He felt better physically since he had eaten, though there was a dull ache at his forehead. Now, he felt another impact of shock. Was Cooper serious? Had his matter-of-fact acceptance of all Mannering had told him and of the situation been a pose? Did he see this as a great opportunity to advance his position with the police? There were a dozen and one possibilities, all crowding upon one another.

"Well," Cooper repeated, "*do* you expect me to let you go?"

"Of course," said Mannering.

"You must understand, Mr. Mannering, that the fact that you are a gentleman of such repute, and that one of the most successful of Scotland Yard's ex-detectives works for you, doesn't give you any special privileges."

"None is needed," Mannering said, and smiled. "If they were, I would certainly expect them."

"Why?" asked Cooper, more coldly.

"Because I've helped the police and co-operated with them for a long time past," Mannering said. "You can play this by the rules and detain me, I suppose, but when you were proved wrong it wouldn't do me any harm and it might do you a lot. However—" He raised his hands, resignedly. "You're in charge, Chief Inspector."

Cooper said levelly: "Have you told me everything, Mr. Mannering?"

"No," answered Mannering.

"Until you have, how can I let you go?"

"You can use your own judgment," Mannering replied. "I really don't want to argue!" He forced a bright smile. "You are wholly responsible. If you lock me up in a cell I shan't try to escape! I would send for my lawyer, of course, and he would—but never mind."

Cooper thrust his underlip forward.

"I want to know *everything*, Mr. Mannering."

"I want my lawyer," Mannering retorted. But he did not like this situation at all, and had a pretty clear idea of what Cooper was thinking. Almost on the instant the policeman proved how right he was, by saying:

"You come here with bloodstains on your hands—you, experienced man who knows better than to touch anything at the scene of a crime—and probably with bloodstains on your clothes. You delayed at least half-an-hour in informing the police and made it difficult for us to question at least one witness. Come, Mr. Mannering! You know I can't let you go. For one thing—" He glanced at Mannering's sleeve. "I want that suit checked for bloodstains and anything else: hairs, for instance."

"Then you must have it," Mannering said obligingly. "But you must charge me first."

"Oh, come!" protested Cooper.

Mannering said much more sharply than he had yet spoken: "What do you expect? That I strip here and now and let you make what tests you have to without a formal charge?" He stood up, pushing the chair back and jolting the tray; a spoon clattered to the floor. "What is it to be? A formal charge? Or may I go?"

Now, he had really forced the issue.

He was a long way from sure what Cooper would do. The man looked both angry and taken aback, although he still controlled himself well. Mannering met his gaze evenly.

There wasn't a thing he could do if he were charged: he would have to stay, and it was even possible that he would be remanded at the magistrates' court hearing, which would have to be held next day. There would be no remand on bail for a man accused of murder. The full significance of this was coming to him heavily, almost frighteningly. And it had come so slowly, step by step, each one quite natural, virtually unavoidable. The simple fact was that Cooper had a *prima facie* case for a charge, which his own lawyer could not possibly dispute. The one thing in his favour was that he had come here voluntarily.

He was utterly in Cooper's hands.

And Cooper, of course, would get in touch with the Yard. The story of the jewels would come out. Gordon would be at his most demanding; Bristow, under pressure, would have to show the letter from Griselda Leo. The more he thought of it the uglier the situation became.

Cooper sat very square and solid in his chair.

"Mr. Mannering," he said, "I am prepared to release you if you will first undergo an examination of your clothes and your hands, but only on condition that you tell me the whole truth. So far I have heard only part of it. If you refuse to tell me the rest then I shall have to charge you, and of course all the examinations will be routine." He pushed his chair back. "I am going to Miss Leo's house. You may have about half-an-hour to consider." He stood up and rounded the desk, adding: "I presume I have your word that you will not leave or attempt to leave."

Mannering, leaning back in his chair, said: "You have."

"Thank you. You may make any telephone calls that you wish," went on Cooper, and he strode out, along the passage, and down the stairs.

.   .   .   .   .

What I have to do, thought Mannering, is to assess the situation as I've never done before. And I have to *think*.

He was suffering slightly from reaction and felt almost light-hearted. In this mood he could see something comical about the way Cooper had stalked out, and the seriousness with which he took the situation. But there wasn't the slightest thing funny about the situation itself. In a way, it was almost as if he were sitting in a cell, awaiting the court hearing.

There was a kind of remorselessness about what had happened. The sequence of events, which in the beginning had seemed accidental and haphazard, now appeared to have a pattern: and the key to the pattern was surely Black Knight.

Now, Mannering really began to think.

First, the letter from Griselda. Then, the discovery that the jewels she had shown in the photographs were stolen. Next, Black Knight's visit and the menaces. Finally, the fact that Black Knight had come here, must have followed him or else been told that he was here.

How much else fitted into the pattern?

Griselda's state of shock?

He had taken to Griselda and trusted her, but now he could imagine that she had sent the letter and the photographs as a blind, that someone—and who but Knight?—had wanted him here. That 'Ted' had been murdered while he had been in the flat so that the evidence would point straight at Mannering.

Well, it couldn't point much straighter!

Could Griselda have been party to such a plot? Could she have fooled him so completely? Had there been the slightest doubt about her joy when he had agreed to advance the money? And could there be any doubt about her being in a state of shock?

He had a sense that if he could find out the truth about

Griselda he might have a key to the puzzle, but he wasn't likely to be able to find out very much. In fact as he was now, he couldn't do very much: he would have to use Bristow and Larraby to help him.

What a start to Bristow's career with him!

He moved nearer the desk, and pulled the telephone towards him—and then he hesitated. If he called Bristow now, would he create difficulties, a conflict of loyalty which would put him, Bristow, in the position of having to make a choice? On the other hand, if he called Josh Larraby and Larraby was able to help without consulting Bristow, then in a way it would be a usurpation of Bristow's new job.

Suddenly, Mannering said aloud: "Confound it, I really am in trouble."

In true emergency he could call on either and both for help, but there was no point at all in creating a difficult situation at Quinns. And he had got himself into this, he ought to be able to get himself out.

He felt a chill run through him.

Griselda had appeared to be taken by surprise, but had she been? Had she been warned that he was coming? If so, who had warned her, and why had she put on such a convincing act of being unprepared?

Of course, Knight could have told her he was in Farnham.

Or—Frank Goodman.

No! That was stretching the long arm of coincidence too far. There was quite enough of a pattern here without coincidence. He needed to follow the pattern, not go out on a limb. And the more he thought the more convinced he became that the key to all of this was Black Knight. He had not named Knight because he had not wanted to involve Griselda more deeply than he must, but she was already involved. And the more he thought, the more reasonable Cooper's ultimatum seemed. He was so used to working by himself that he objected almost by habit to such demands; that didn't make him right this time.

He lifted the receiver, and at once an operator said: "Can I help you, sir?"

"Get me Chelsea 3214, will you," Mannering said. "That's my wife."

"I'll call you back," the man promised.

Mannering stood at the window, waiting for the call. The orchard beyond the walls was touched with the afterglow; so was the narrow river, running silently by. A scent of new-mown hay came wafting from the orchard. As night fell the sky was cloudless and the stars very bright.

The bell rang, and he picked the receiver up quickly.

"Your wife, sir."

"Thank you ... Lorna!" said Mannering, infusing some feeling into his voice. "Did you get my message?"

"Yes, darling," Lorna said, quite matter-of-fact. "What happened so quickly?"

"Oh, just a little trifle like being suspected of murder," Mannering said.

"John, don't joke," she protested.

"It's no joke," Mannering assured her, still lightly, and he heard Lorna catch her breath. "I don't think we need worry, darling, but I do need a suit and a pair of shoes. Can you bring them out to Farnham police station?"

After a pause, Lorna said: "Of course. It will take me an hour or more, but I'll start straightaway." After another pause, she added: "It *isn't* anything to worry about, is it?"

Mannering said: "I don't think so. I'll tell you all about it when you get here."

He rang off, and wiped the back of his neck, considered, and then plucked up the telephone again. It was madness not to tell Bristow what had happened; Bristow must decide what he could and would do, and if there was a limit to how far he could commit himself, then the sooner they both realised it the better. He gave the operator Bristow's number, and this time waited for what seemed a long time, before the bell rang sharply.

It was the operator.

"The number's engaged, sir. Shall I keep on trying?"

"Yes, please," Mannering said, putting the receiver down.

At least he had plenty of time to think.

Now, he began to concentrate on the jewels. They had been there, they had been genuine, and worth that fifty thousand pounds. When he had gone rushing after Black Knight, they had been on the table, but had they been there when he had come back?

He couldn't be sure. He had been so concerned with Griselda.

He went over each one of his movements very carefully. The jewels had been there when the man had run down the stairs. They had not been there after he had returned from speaking to the burly man downstairs. They could have disappeared during the time he had been at the car, and—Griselda herself could have taken them and hidden them.

Could anyone else have done so?

There was no way of being sure that no one had been up to 47d while he had been talking to the police and the crowd outside the gates. He must have been there for at least twenty minutes, ample time for someone from the crowd to have slipped into the garden, gone round to 47d, and sneaked upstairs. He had not been watching the gate all the time. But, only someone who had known there was something worth stealing would have gone upstairs.

Who knew?

Did Goodman?

He hadn't seen Goodman but that didn't mean the man hadn't been there. There was no certainty that Black

Knight hadn't had someone in the crowd, too.

But why would Black Knight's man have reason to think it worth raiding the apartment?

The simple truth was that the most likely person to have moved those jewels was Griselda Leo. There might have been someone hiding at the flat but it was impossible. Griselda had had plenty of time to hide them; for all he knew, she might still have them in a pocket or a handbag. The trouble was that he could not imagine how the girl, in her shocked state, could have behaved rationally.

Well: why need she have been rational? The jewels were obviously of such importance to her that, back in the apartment and seeing them on the table, her first, almost instinctive, reaction might have been to put them somewhere safe.

The telephone bell rang. Ah: this would be Bristow.

"Your Putney call," the operator said, and then came Bristow's voice, brisk and businesslike:

"Who is that?"

"John Mannering," said Mannering.

"Good lord!" exclaimed Bristow, and after a pause he added: "I thought you were under arrest! I've just been wondering whether to tell Lorna you've run into trouble, or whether to come to Farnham myself."

"She's on her way with a change of clothes," Mannering said. "Bill—how did you find out?"

"Gordon told me. I've only just come off the phone with him," answered Bristow. "Apparently he warned the Farnham police that you might be going there and suggested they kept an eye on you. And apparently he knows the man in charge there, Cooper. Cooper telephoned and told him how right he'd been. Ian told me as much as he knew. How serious is it, John?"

Before Mannering could answer, he went on: "And what can I do?" He gave a little, half-embarrassed laugh. "I'm sorry you're in trouble, but if I can help you out of it as my first job, I'd really feel I was worth my keep!"

12

ANGRY YOUNG MAN

Mannering felt a curious contraction at his heart; a sense not far from guilt. He had been so full of doubts and Bristow was so full of loyalty. In fact, it was almost funny. Yet it was a warning, too, and it taught him that he could not make a clear judgment of others although he knew them so well. He had always been reasonably sure what Bristow would do as a policeman: now he knew what he would do as manager of Quinns.

But it did not alter the fact that he, Mannering, must not let Bristow run into trouble for him.

"Are you there?" asked Bristow.

"Yes, Bill," Mannering said slowly. "Is that really how you feel?"

"How would you expect me to feel?" There was a fractional pause before Bristow went on: "I've worked with and against you for so long that I'd support you against the official view at any time. You'd be surprised how often I've wished I could come out on your side, when I was at the Yard. Now, I can. Do you mean they've had the sense *not* to make a formal charge?"

"I'm to be searched and my clothes analysed. Then if I'm a good boy I can come home."

"You sound too meek to be true," Bristow said with a chuckle. "Is there anything I can do for you by telephone? Or here in town?"

After a moment, Mannering said: "Do you still play

chess?"

"Chess?" Bristow sounded puzzled.

"The game," Mannering explained. "Kings and queens and knights and—"

"*Ahhh!*" breathed Bristow. "Now I've got you. This morning's little game of chess at Quinns, you mean? The black piece."

"That's it," Mannering said. "I'd like it very much."

"Oh," said Bristow, gruffly. "I can't say it will be easy to find, but I'll try. Are you sure it's the right piece?"

"Positive," asserted Mannering.

"Leave it to me," said Bristow, as if with great confidence.

Mannering rang off, smiling; he felt better than he had for a long time. Bristow had been very quick, and his early remarks had been for the ears of the police: now Cooper would be in no doubt what Bristow felt. *Ahhh!* Bristow had breathed. *Ah!* He leaned back in the chair, which was surprisingly comfortable, and closed his eyes. Mental pictures still entered his mind but they no longer flashed, they were in slow motion. Griselda was the only one who stayed clear, the only one for whom he felt any concern.

Could she have lied?

Could she?

Could—she—have—lied?

He was aware of a faraway feeling, rare for him, and yet he felt that he was awake. He had no idea how long he had been dozing when he heard a sound, opened his eyes slowly and saw Cooper at the other side of the desk, looking down at him. There was humour in Cooper's eyes despite the sarcasm in his voice.

"That comes of having an easy conscience, does it?"

"Shouldn't be surprised," Mannering said, straightening up. On the instant his mind cleared and sleep seemed to vanish. "How is Griselda?"

Cooper said with great clarity: "She is in hospital, no

doubt under sedation."

"Oh," said Mannering. "Good." He sat erect, and asked: "Did you find anything worthwhile?"

"Everything was exactly as you told us," said Cooper. "The doctor was with her and refused to allow us to question her. She was, and is, suffering very severely from shock. What would you have expected us to find?"

"Some diamond and emerald jewellery," answered Mannering.

Now, Cooper smiled quite broadly.

"So you've decided to come clean?"

"Yes," Mannering said. "I decided that it wasn't worth making a lot of fuss and trouble because I came here to see Griselda Leo about some antique jewellery." He took a letter from his inside breast pocket and handed it across. "I saw the jewels, and identified them. Knowing they were stolen I wouldn't make an offer or accept them as security so I offered the money against other valuables, which—"

"Might also prove to have been stolen," Cooper put in quickly.

"It's conceivable," Mannering agreed. "If they are and were covered by insurance then I would expect to get most of my money back. If they weren't covered—" He shrugged and smiled brightly. "I can take risks with my own money, surely?"

"From what I gather of you, you'll take risks with your own life. One of these days you may lose it."

"We all take risks," Mannering said solemnly.

Cooper leaned back, so that his weight was on the two back legs of his chair, and looked about to comment. He was a very powerful man physically, and very strong-willed. Instead of commenting, he said briskly:

"I would like a written statement."

"I'll do it while I'm waiting for my wife, who's coming with a change of clothes," Mannering said.

"I understood you'd telephoned her," Cooper responded drily.

He made no mention of having heard the call to Bristow but there was little doubt that he knew about that, also.

He gave Mannering some plain paper and Mannering wrote his statement quickly, omitting only that he had recognised Black Knight. When he had finished he knew that he had created a great deal of circumstantial evidence against Griselda, but he did not see how it was avoidable. It was after ten-thirty by the time he had finished, and quite dark. The police station was remarkably quiet, only a few men moved about but he could hear cars coming to and fro in the courtyard. The ring of the telephone startled him, and he hesitated before answering, but at last lifted the receiver.

"Mrs. Mannering is downstairs, sir," the operator said.

"Ah, thanks. Is Chief Inspector Cooper in?"

"He said if he wasn't back before you left, would you please leave your address. Oh—and you could change in his office."

"He's very helpful," Mannering said. "Will you have my wife shown up?"

When Lorna came, she looked a little dishevelled, more than a little anxious, but they didn't say a word about what had happened until he had changed and was ready to go. Mannering had an odd feeling of relief as he nodded to the policeman at the entrance, and went to Lorna's car, a Morris 1800. As she started the engine Mannering had a flash of alarm: he could almost see the bonnet of the Aston Martin billowing flame and smoke.

"Straight home?" asked Lorna.

"No. There's a dealer named Goodman I'd like to see." He told her about Frank Goodman, the bronze lion and the speed with which the man had come to help Griselda.

She drew up outside the bow-shaped window. The shop itself was in darkness but a light showed through the fanlight above the front door. Mannering rang, and almost at once footsteps sounded. The door opened, and Goodman appeared. He seemed to draw back, but did not move more than a few inches, and his voice was harsh.

"Oh, it's you."

Mannering said: "I've just been released from the police station, and before going back to London I want to make sure Miss Leo is as well as she can be."

"If she is, it's no thanks to you," Goodman said. Then he stepped forward and a trick of the light shadowed his eyes and gave him a vicious, sinister look. "If anything happens to her I'll make you pay. I'll make you pay if it ruins me."

Very quietly, Mannering asked: "What's made you feel like this?"

"Don't be a bloody hypocrite!" Goodman shouted, and his voice echoed up and down the street. "You killed her uncle and stole those jewels. My God, I could wring your neck this minute!"

Two people stopped to stare.

Along the street a policeman watched; he must have heard every syllable.

At the wheel of the car, Lorna waited.

Mannering did not speak, but quite suddenly moved forward, pushing Goodman's arm aside as the man tried to stop him. He said roughly:

"How do you know about the jewels? Come on! Tell me." And when Goodman didn't reply he went on in the same rough voice: "Tell me or the police, I don't care which. *What do you know about the jewels?*"

Goodman was pressing against the wall, looking for a moment as if he hardly knew what had happened. Then his expression changed and he launched himself at Mannering. He was much younger than Mannering, and if he knew anything about in-fighting such an assault would be deadly. As he came on, arms flailing, Mannering gripped his right arm and twisted, so that suddenly Goodman was facing the open door, with his right arm thrust up behind him in a hammer-lock. Over his shoulder Mannering saw first Lorna, then a policeman, who seemed too startled to move.

"What do you know about the jewels?" Mannering hissed into his ear, and thrust his arm up far enough to hurt.

The policeman was still watching. Goodman was gasping, and his body was taut as steel.

"Tell me!" rasped Mannering.

"Griselda—Griselda told me."

"When did she tell you?"

"Tonight. When—when I got there." Goodman had the sense not to move against the pressure, and he did not protest. Sweat was beginning to trickle down the side of his face.

"She wasn't capable of saying anything," Mannering growled.

"When—when I got there she was. She said there were some jewels, she'd shown them to you, and they'd gone."

"I tell you she wasn't capable of saying anything."

"She gasped it out," Goodman gasped in turn. "At first I hardly realised what she was saying. She stammered every word, I had to string them together."

"And then you jumped to conclusions," Mannering growled, letting him go.

Goodman moved his arm and shoulder about as he turned to face Mannering. He was sweating freely now, there was little doubt he had been afraid that Mannering would break his arm.

"Well, you were there, weren't you? And she did show you the jewels. And they *have* gone. I hope the police searched you thoroughly. I'd strip you if I had my way."

"Goodman," Mannering said. "I didn't touch those jewels."

"I don't believe you."

"You'd better believe me if you want to help Griselda."

"What do you mean?" Goodman stopped wriggling his shoulders.

"I mean that either someone else stole them, or Griselda hid them."

Mannering was completely unprepared for Goodman's reaction. The man simply drew back his left arm then clenched his fist and smashed at Mannering's chin. Mannering had just time to move his head and avoid the full force of the blow but it was powerful enough to knock him off his balance. Lorna came running and the policeman called, "That's enough!" as he followed her.

But Goodman made no attempt to launch a second blow. As Lorna pushed past, he said sneeringly:

"The bloody swine! Trying to put the blame on a woman. Get that man out of my house. I don't ever want to see him again."

"Do you want to make a charge, Mr. Goodman?" the policeman asked.

"I'll leave that to you—when you've got the evidence against him," Goodman growled.

Mannering's chin was sore but he wasn't hurt seriously. He heard everything Goodman said but made no attempt to argue with him. Lorna led the way out of the house and held open the door of her car. Mannering got in, rubbing his chin. As Lorna took the wheel, he laughed.

"That will teach me to deal with young men in love."

"Didn't you realise how he felt?" asked Lorna.

"I had an idea he worshipped from afar, but I thought he'd be eager for me to help." He laughed again. "But there's something odd about it. When I saw Griselda last she was incapable of speech and she must still be pretty bad, they've taken her to hospital and put her under sedation."

"Darling." Lorna said, starting the engine, "don't fool yourself about that young man, will you. You insulted the woman he loves and he had a caveman reaction. It was really rather magnificent. That is, it would have been if you hadn't been the victim," she added hastily.

"Magnificent is one word," Mannering said. "Are you sure he's not being very clever? I mean, putting on an act?"

"If he is, it's a very convincing act," Lorna said. She was silent while she watched for one-way streets and the signs to London, but once they were on the by-pass, she asked: "Can you bear to tell me about it?"

He told her. She was obviously shaken, obviously worried. They were going fast along the Guildford by-pass, beyond Guildford, when she asked:

"It isn't very healthy, is it?"

"I've known worse situations," said Mannering.

"I don't know," replied Lorna. "This has a nasty sneaky feeling, as if everything has crept up from behind you. Are you sure the murderer was Black Knight?"

"I'm sure that the man running down the stairs was," said Mannering. "And the odds that he killed Griselda's Uncle Ted are pretty high. But it could have been someone else. I suppose it could have been someone else who put the nitroglycerine under the bonnet of my car, too." He sat in silence for a while, beginning to fret a little because he wasn't driving, but in many ways he could think more clearly while Lorna drove with casual skill. Suddenly, he said: "I went to Goodman's shop because I saw a piece of china I thought might be Ming, but it wasn't. Only after I'd bought the lion—"

"Lion?" interrupted Lorna.

"Oh, lord, I forgot. I bought a Gougon bronze lion and

put it in the back of my car. I suppose it will be all right."
He considered for a moment before going on: "It *was* sheer
chance I went there at all. He obviously knew a lot about
Griselda but I can't believe he's involved in any way. Yet
if he was putting on an act, now, he *is* involved."

"He isn't putting up an act," said Lorna. "He's desperately in love."

"Woman's intuition," suggested Mannering, almost
tartly.

"No, darling. Woman's observation." She passed a slow-
moving milk tanker, and went on: "So Bill Bristow didn't
hesitate about throwing his hat over the windmill."

"It was the best moment I've had tonight when I realised
how he reacted," Mannering said. "I wonder if he's had
any luck locating Black Knight."

"He hasn't had time," Lorna said. "John—"

"Yes?"

"Do you think the girl's letter and Black Knight's visit
were related?"

"That's one of the possibilities that haunt me," he said
ruefully.

They fell silent. He was aware that Lorna was paying
great attention to the driving-mirror but as they neared
London there was much more traffic about. There was a
steady stream coming home, and conditions were trying for
driving. He wished he were at the wheel when Lorna began
to pull over to one side, and then drew into the kerb.

"I'm not sure," she said, "but I think we're being followed. You'll be able to tell better if you drive."

He got out and took the wheel as Lorna shifted over,
then moved carefully into a stream of traffic. At first so
many cars were behind that it was impossible to be sure,
but soon after they came onto the Staines by-pass, near
Runnymede, he was certain that a small car with very
bright headlamps was trailing them.

He put on speed, slackened, swung into different lanes, but all the time the other car kept close behind; and it was still near them when they reached Chelsea, three-quarters of an hour later, and turned off King's Road into Green Street, where the Mannerings lived. It passed the end of the street, and Mannering pulled into a parking place near the front door of their building.

"We'll wait and see if the car turns up," he said, and switched off both the engine and the lights.

As he did so, and they gradually became accustomed to the light from tall, old-fashioned street lamps, a man moved from the entrance to the house where they lived, and came briskly towards them.

It was Bristow.

13

BLACK NEWS

Bristow leaned inside the car as Lorna opened the window and said: "Well, I must say you didn't dawdle. Hallo, Lorna —it didn't take him long to embroil me into a case, did it?" Without giving her time to answer, he went on: "I don't know what to advise, John—that you go in and hope for the best, or hide for a while." He looked at Lorna. "Sorry to have put it so crudely."

"What's happened now?" Mannering asked quietly.

"They've found four of the jewels," Bristow told him.

"Where?"

"In the boot of your car, at the garage."

Mannering sat absolutely still. Lorna put a hand on his knee, and said: "Oh, darling."

"I can tell you something else," Bristow went on.

"The worst, please," said Mannering.

"Your prints are on the murder weapon. The dead man's blood is on your jacket and trousers. Several of his hairs were found on the sleeves of your jacket, too. You had the opportunity, and the fact that the jewels were found in your car shows a strong motivation. And, John—" Bristow paused, as both of them looked at his face, pale in the lamplight: only his eyes seemed bright.

"Yes?"

"You haven't a friend at court, this time."

With an effort, Lorna asked: "You mean at the Yard?"

"I mean at the Yard," confirmed Bristow.

The pressure of Lorna's hand on Mannering's knee grew firmer.

Neither of them would advise him; no one knew him better. He could go away and hide; he had a car, garaged under another name, and he could change his appearance enough to make sure he wasn't recognised except under the closest scrutiny. But if he ran in this particular case, it would be tantamount to admitting guilt; or at least, fear.

A small car with very bright headlights turned into the street from the far end, the Embankment. The lights dimmed, and the car crawled past. The driver was a young man whom Mannering did not recognise; he pulled in a few yards behind Mannering's car on the other side of the road.

"Where did you learn this?" Mannering asked Bristow.

"Gordon."

"So he's being co-operative."

"John," said Bristow, "I don't think so. I think he's making sure you know what's going on because he think's you'll go into hiding. Then there'll be a hue and cry. He reasons that he will catch you, and thus put himself in line for promotion." Bristow uttered each word with great care; almost as if they hurt his lips. "Don't get me wrong. He's first and foremost a policeman. He knows this case goes back in history, that the stolen gems were being kept at the Leo woman's home, that you were interested in them, and so, he argues, open to a deal, the more so as they've been out of circulation for so long. He sees this as a big case with a lot of ramifications and he'll use every trick in the book to break it. And he thinks he'll be well on the way to do this if you cut and run."

After a long, broody pause, Mannering asked: "Have you any idea where Black Knight is?"

"No. And I'm pretty sure they don't know at the Yard. I'm even more sure that the police will cover any place they think he might be, both to get him and to catch you. I can go on looking for him, but you can't."

"I see," said Mannering, heavily. "Cleft stick for me."

"Do you think they'll charge John with the murder if they were to have him in custody now?" asked Lorna.

"They're much more likely to charge him with being in possession of the jewels, knowing them to have been stolen."

"Would he get bail for that?" asked Lorna. Her hand was burning into Mannering's knee.

"Not if the police opposed it," said Bristow. "I think they probably wouldn't oppose. They'd like to have John on a piece of string, expecting him to make some move which would incriminate him much more."

"I don't understand," objected Lorna.

Mannering put his hand over hers, gently.

"It isn't too difficult," he said. "The Ottenshaw robbery was a very big one. And Black Knight took part in a lot of other big ones, too. It's reasonable to think I've been buying and selling some of the loot, that I'm involved up to my neck in it. Isn't that about right, Bill?" he asked grimly.

"It's what I would have thought a few years ago," answered Bristow. "I might even have suspected it up to a few months ago. I would have credited you with lily-white motives, of course!" There was an edge of anxiety to his voice. "I'm afraid one thing's certain, John."

"What particular thing?"

"Once you're indoors, they'll keep tabs on you, and you won't have a chance of getting away. I haven't seen anyone here yet, except the man who pulled in ten minutes ago, but you can be pretty sure Gordon's having the place watched."

"Yes," said Mannering. "Yes." He drew a deep breath. "Well, I'm going indoors. I need a good night's sleep if I'm to face tomorrow." His voice brightened. "Have you told Larraby that we want Black Knight?"

"Yes. He's put his feelers out, too, John. If we get a squeak, we'll let you know."

"Good," said Mannering. "If I should be placed under house arrest, we need to know all we can about Black Knight, Frank Goodman, Griselda Leo and her Uncle Ted. The more we know about them all the better chance we'll have."

"Right," said Bristow. "I—"

He broke off, drew his head out of the window and peered along the street. There was tension in his attitude as he watched a car coming along very slowly. Mannering glanced into his wing mirror, and saw the 'Police' sign on top of the car. There were five men in it. Three of them got out and as the car moved off these men took up positions in the doorways of houses nearby. The driver of the car which had followed Mannering and Lorna from Farnham got out of his seat and went to one of the new arrivals. It was impossible to hear what was being said, but the man moved briskly away and stepped into his car and drove off.

"A Farnham policeman," Bristow said, stiffly.

"Keeping an eye on the bad man," Mannering replied with forced lightness.

"There's another police car at the end of the street," Bristow said. "John, I'm afraid—" He broke off.

"Blocked in," said Mannering.

"Oh, my darling!" exclaimed Lorna.

"Well, there's still a chance of getting that good night's sleep!" Mannering said, the heartiness only slightly forced. "Thanks. Bill." He got out of the car as Bristow opened the opposite door for Lorna, locked all the doors and joined them on the pavement. No one else made sound or movement but the night seemed full of watching eyes. "One other thing," Mannering went on.

"Yes?" said Bristow.

"Don't get yourself into trouble over me whatever you do."

"Well, obviously I won't if I can help it," Bristow replied.

"I mean absolutely," Mannering said. "Don't take risks, Bill. And don't assume that I'm being quixotic. If this affair goes wrong, and it very well could, I need someone reliable at Quinns."

Lorna drew in her breath sharply.

"And if I should be charged and then committed for trial, there will be several months' wait before the assizes. Everything has to be kept ticking over, and I'll need someone digging for Black Knight. Don't do anything to get yourself in bad odour with the Yard. I really mean it."

"Bill," said Lorna, "you mustn't take any risks."

"I see what you mean," said Bristow, gruffly. "I won't stick my neck out. But I'll do my damnedest—" He broke off, waving his hands. "Well, you know."

"I know," agreed Mannering, and then raised his voice slightly. "That's what we'll do then, Bill. And I'll see you at the shop in the morning. Good night."

Bristow echoed: "Good night," and turned and stalked off.

The Mannerings went towards their flat, in one of the three houses left in the Georgian terrace, and found the small lift on the ground floor. There was just room for them. It crawled upwards, and they didn't speak. At the third and top floor, Mannering got out first; there was always a chance of something unpleasant awaiting them: Black Knight, for instance.

The narrow landing was empty.

Mannering unlocked the front door, switched on lights, and they went into room after room. The dining-room and kitchen, the drawing room, Mannering's study, their bedroom, a small spare room, and two bathrooms. He put on all the lights, then went along a narrow passage outside

one bathroom. Above their heads was the big loft used as
Lorna's studio, the latch closed now, the long loft ladder
fastened to the wall. If any one were hiding, it would
be there.

"I think I'll check," Mannering said.

Lorna nodded. She seemed too tense to speak.

Mannering lowered the ladder with a pulley which also
operated the hatch cover, and switched on lights from
downstairs. Soon he was in the studio, a huge, raftered
and beamed room, with two easels standing, half-finished
portraits on each, and dozens of pictures, without frames,
lining the walls. There was an odour of oil paint and tur-
pentine, quite strong because the studio had been closed
up for much of the day.

On one side was an alcove where Lorna mixed her paints;
and on one of several paint-daubed shelves stood a theatri-
cal make-up box which Mannering had used often in the
past. He could sit at this table, open the box, and change
his appearance so that no one would recognise him, in little
more than half-an-hour.

Lorna called: "Darling!"

He called back: "Coming!"

"Is everything all right?"

"It is up here!" He backed nimbly down the ladder, and
found Lorna coming from the kitchen. She was pale and
obviously worried, and very slowly put her arms around
him. They stood for what seemed a long time, and he knew
that she was crying and yet trying to keep back tears.

They had known crises like this, some even worse, but
there had never been such poignancy. Partly it was because this had happened with such little warning; partly, it
was because they had had their own emotional problems
in the past few years, and had come through to deeper
understanding, and so deeper love, than ever. All this was
evident in the tightness of her hold.

At last, she drew away, smiling.

"I'm sorry."

"It was rather nice," Mannering said with forced lightness.

"John, don't joke."

"That wasn't a joke."

They moved, hand in hand, into the study: he could hear an electric kettle, singing: it was almost automatic for one of them to make tea as soon as they came home.

"I have such an awful feeling of impending doom." Lorna tried to sound facetious but failed hopelessly. "I know I should be all bright and cheerful but—darling, I really am frightened. It's all been done so—so cleverly. One thing after another happens and makes the situation a little worse."

"I know exactly what you mean," said Mannering.

"So you feel like that, too."

"In a way," Mannering agreed. "I feel—" The click of the kettle going off the boil sounded and he started towards the kitchen, small, very modern and bright. He pushed the control lever in again: a loaded tea-tray was standing in readiness, and he warmed the pot. "I feel that I could do the wrong thing and really be in trouble."

She nodded.

"I could stay, and let things take their course," Mannering went on musingly. "That's virtually what I've been doing since it began. Or—" He broke off.

"You can put on a disguise, and go out and fight," she said, heavily.

"Yes."

"Could you really get away from here?"

"Oh yes, over the rooftops."

He made the tea, a most commonplace act, as he talked about taking a risk which would daunt almost any man. Lorna picked up the tray and looked into his hazel brown eyes; hers were so clear a grey.

"John, I think you should go."

"*You* think so?" he exclaimed.

"I know, I usually hate it when you take chances, but— I don't really see that you've any choice."

She was making sure that he did not draw back because of her, and he warmed towards her. For the first time since he had gone to Farnham, his heart felt lighter. He had been pushed around by a series of circumstances quite beyond his control, and he was never at his best when on the defensive. If he could turn to the attack he might be able to find the truth long before anyone else; he might be the only man who could find the truth.

"Bless you," he said. "I haven't any choice, have I? I'll have this cup of tea and then go and get ready."

He sat drinking tea as calmly as if it were a most ordinary of nights—despite the waiting, watching police and the strong chain of circumstantial evidence and, hovering almost as if he were in the room, the bearded figure of Black Knight.

Twenty minutes later, Mannering went up to the studio again.

He was wearing only an undervest and underpants as he hitched himself up on a stool by the make-up mirror, and began to work on his face. For the first few minutes his movements were slow and deliberate, it was so long since he had done this. But gradually his old expertise returned. He cleansed his face, worked the greasepaint into his skin, put quick-setting glue at the corners of his eyes, to narrow them, etched lines at mouth and nose and forehead.

With every move, his appearance changed.

He grew less and less like John Mannering until at last, he seemed to disappear absolutely as Mannering and to become another man, one with a pasty face, wrinkles, and the bloated nose and cheeks of a heavy drinker.

He worked a thin plastic covering over his teeth, top and bottom, and they appeared to be yellowed and tobacco-stained and bigger than his own. Every now and again he paused to examine himself closely, and become more and more satisfied. He took an eye dropper and dipped it into a tiny bottle of liquid which did not cause pain but made the eyes look bloodshot. Then finally he put suction pads into his mouth to draw in his cheeks and make him look almost haggard.

He stood up, quickly, and then wound a serpent-like tube about his waist, and inflated it with an airbed inflator. This added inches to his waist. Next, he coiled a length of nylon cord beneath this. Next, he took a waistcoat from a drawer and slipped it on. It hunched his back and made his shoulders slope; he was not even remotely the man who had entered here less than half-an-hour before.

He called down to Lorna, who began to come up, while he examined the narrow window through which he would soon climb out onto the roof. There was an easy way over the roof to the house next door, but the police would be watching that; tonight he had to go the difficult way.

14

ROOFTOP

"John," Lorna said, "what are you going to do?"

"Find Black Knight," Mannering answered.

"Have you any idea where he is?"

Mannering lied with utmost conviction, because he knew how desperately she needed hope to cling to.

"I have an idea, yes."

"Where?" Immediately she was eager. "Can Bristow help? Or Josh, or—"

He slid his arms round her and kissed her to silence, and as he drew away said: "It's a job I must start for myself."

She struggled with her fears, and finally made herself say lightly:

"Well, at least you'll take some chocolate and biscuits with you." She pushed a flat package into his pocket.

"Bless you," Mannering said. "Good night, my love."

He turned away immediately to the narrow window. He was aware of Lorna for a few seconds but almost at once he had to concentrate on the task ahead. He dared not dwell on her or on anything: he had to take this affair step by step, and the next one was to get out onto the roof. He could not be seen from the street but there were vantage points on the roofs opposite and on one side; the police might have stationed men there.

He edged out, sideways.

He had used this window often in the past, and had strengthened the ledge and straightened and flattened some slates, so as to tread safely. And the window was behind thick chimney stacks, invisible from any vantage spot. He reached the stack. The night was star-bright and very clear. He studied the roofs and was sure no one watched from them. Now, crouching, he left the shelter of the stack and for a few moments was visible from the street, and would be seen if anyone looked up. He crouched, bent almost double, and went from this roof to the next and the shelter of the neighbouring stack.

He reached it—and a slate cracked beneath him.

The report seemed sharp and loud. He stood absolutely still, listening. Cars hummed on the Embankment and along King's Road but he heard neither voices nor footsteps.

A man coughed, and sneezed; then silence settled.

Mannering crossed the next roof. This was not made secure and he had to walk much more gingerly, but he crossed it without trouble. An aeroplane droned, and he could see its red and green navigation lights. He reached the last of the three tall houses, and edged along the side of the roof towards the corner of the house at the back. His flat would be watched from the back, of course, but at this corner the chances of being seen were negligible.

Now, he had to climb down.

The old houses had ornamented brickwork, offering footholds almost as good as an escape ladder. Years ago he had known them well, using this way of getting in and out of the flat unobserved. But the years made a great difference, and as with the make-up, he was out of practice. There were four floors; if he slipped and fell he might kill himself, or at best break a leg or an arm.

He had a mental picture of Uncle Ted, sprawled on the staircase.

He lay full length on the coping, the slate roof slanting up towards the chimney blotting out the stars, and peered down. The ornamented ledges were still there; of course they were, what the hell was the matter with him? He edged a little further, and then lowered himself over, legs first. The rough ledge scraped his knees but he did not stop. He grated his elbow on the guttering, in which water glistened. Slowly, slowly, he kept edging over until he was hanging onto the ledge at full length, swinging, groping with his feet for the nearest foothold.

The man below sneezed again, a sudden sound which made Mannering start. A car turned into Green Street, engine sounding very loud.

He felt the foothold he was groping for, and cautiously trusted some of his weight to it; it held.

He gave himself a moment's rest before going further. Here and there among the houses were the bright squares of lighted windows, one of them almost on a level with him.

Pressing close against the wall, he stretched his left arm towards another ledge, touched it, and eased some of his weight onto it. He was like a giant crab, crawling downwards. But he was more used to it now, and every foot he moved he drew a little nearer safety.

He went down easily and quickly and was soon within a comparatively safe dropping distance. Well, he wouldn't lose his foothold now; he was as safe as—

A light flashed out from a window at his side. One moment there was all darkness about him, next, a brilliant light shone on a garden, a fence, trees and bushes. And someone moved inside the room.

Had he been seen or heard?

If he had, then the next few moments would show.

He heard a click of sound, realised that a man or woman was drinking; the light went off as abruptly as it had come on. Mannering's heart was still thumping, but he started down again, and at last his foot touched earth. Both feet

planted firmly on the ground, he stood silently, listening.
All seemed well. He had only one wall to climb and he
would be in the street which ran parallel to Green Street.
He peered over the wall first, saw no one, hauled himself
up and over, and walked rapidly towards King's Road.

No one stopped or watched him.

He turned left, towards Fulham, for he had a lock-up
garage and a car in a side street not far from Lots Road
Power Station, only twenty minutes' walk from here. He
passed the end of Green Street, and caught a glimpse of
two of the policemen watching his house. He gave an ex-
plosive little laugh as he walked on.

For the first time for many years he was on the run from
the police. And now that he had won the first round a
kind exhilaration grew. He felt younger, eager, confident.

After all, he simply had to find Black Knight!

Soon, he turned along the narrow street where the car
was garaged. A street lamp shone close to it and several
square windows at the little houses showed light. The garages were in an alley off the street, and he thought he saw
a man's shadow. He slackened his pace. From the other end
of the street a small car came, only its sidelights on; the
head and shoulders of a couple in it showed almost as one.
Small cars and motor cycles covered with nylon sheets like
shrouds, were parked on either side. He drew near the
alley, and paused.

A girl said: "I've got to go, Dave."

A sound which might have been a kiss followed.

Then: "Oh, Dave." And soon: "Dave, I've got to go, my
Dad will carry on something awful if I don't."

Mannering, in the shadows of the house on the corner,
waited for what seemed an age before the couple, arms en-
twined, moved. 'Dave' was half-a-head shorter than the girl,
who had an enormous mop of hair and looked as if she

had just come from a hair-dressing *salon*. They vanished at last and Mannering went into the alley and to the door of the garage. There were three garages, of wood with corrugated iron roofs, each one locked with hasp and padlock. He took out his keys and took the padlock between the fingers of his right hand, to steady it.

It came away in his hand. This padlock had been forced.

He stood absolutely still, the various possibilities passing through his mind. The police could have found this and be waiting inside. Or the car might have been stolen. Or vandals might have broken in, bent on practising their savage cult of destruction.

Then he heard a whisper from the other side of the door.

"It's all right, sir. It's me. Josh Larraby."

And Larraby opened one of the doors for Mannering to get in, and then closed it, with hardly a sound.

. . . . .

"I hope I didn't scare you, sir?"

"Just frightened the life out of me, that's all!" Mannering gasped.

"I'm *very* sorry, sir."

"Don't be. I'd forgotten you knew about this car."

"It's a long time ago since you told me," Larraby replied.

It was indeed; and Larraby was the only man in the world who knew about this place and the big, old-fashioned car which nearly filled the garage. There was enough room to stand at the front, and two wooden benches. Mannering shivered as he sat down; it was chilly. He had once left some 'borrowed' jewels here and he had not been able to collect them himself at the time, being shadowed by the police. So he had sent Josh.

"How did you know I was coming here?" asked Mannering. "Did my wife—"

"I thought it was the most likely place," Larraby interrupted.

"Does Bristow know you're looking for me?"

"No. I thought I should keep this to myself. In any case I wasn't sure whether he knew about this place."

"He doesn't." Mannering leaned back against the rough wooden sides, and something metallic rattled. "Why did you come, Josh?"

"I'm sure you know the general details," said Larraby, "and that the situation is very dangerous. A general call has gone out to all police stations, about you. It says that the Farnham police would like you to help them in their enquiries."

"The sinister note," Mannering said. "I do know, Josh. And if it gets into the newspapers there will be only one interpretation." Larraby would have learned what he knew from his friends on the other side of the law, for he had contacts all over London. "What else?"

"I've learned something about Knight, sir, which I think you ought to know."

"*Ah!*" breathed Mannering. "What is it?"

"I think the best thing would be for you to hear that at first hand," Larraby answered. "I've located his first wife, and she hasn't any love for him."

"Where is she?" asked Mannering.

"She lives in Islington, sir, Kitt Street, and she's prepared for a visit from you . . ."

⋆   ⋆   ⋆

Islington, not far from the heart of London, to the north, has a mass of Victorian houses behind the proud new façade of modern shops and apartment blocks. The streets were brightly lit as Mannering drove on Larraby's instructions. Now and again a policeman looked at them curiously, once a police car seemed to trail them for half a mile, but it led to no further alarm. Kitt Street was a short thoroughfare of three-storey terrace houses which looked very narrow. In four of them lights showed at glass panels in the front doors, and Larraby said:

"The second lighted house, sir."

There was room to park a few doors along, and soon they stood together in a cubicle of a porch. Their presence seemed to add a strange furtiveness to the scene. Presently footsteps sounded inside the house, and a small woman opened the door.

"I'm back, Mrs. Knight," Larraby said.

"I've got eyes," the woman retorted. "Come in." She led them along a passage towards a narrow dining-room which led off the kitchen; a green chenille cloth was spread over a table, a flourishing azalea plant in the exact centre. The place was spotless: here was an extremely house-proud woman. The big chairs had stuffed backs and arms. Small easy chairs were grouped at one end of the room, and she motioned to them.

"Anyone like a beer?" she asked.

"A very good idea," Mannering approved.

"I would indeed," answered Larraby.

The woman nodded and went into the kitchen. She was small-boned, with a slender waist and nicely-shaped legs. When she came back, carrying three bottles of beer and three glasses on a tray, the centre light showed how grey her hair was, showed up some of the lines on her face. Young, she must have been elfin-pretty. Now, the lines of bitterness at her lips were unmistakable.

"I don't know who you are but I do know Josh works for Mr. Mannering," she said, "and I know Blackie's after Mannering's blood. I know Blackie, all right." She raised her glass. "Cheers."

Almost as if they were drinking a toast, they all drank.

Mannering's light beer was exactly what he needed: sharp and biting as well as cold.

"Why is he after Mr. Mannering?" Mannering asked. He spoke in a voice very different from his natural one; almost Cockney.

"Mannering put him inside. He swore he'd get him, and if Blackie says he'll do a thing, he'll do it." There was a kind of reluctant admiration in her voice. "He was on the run, and came here. That blonde bitch he was living with, he didn't want to get her in trouble but he didn't care what happened to me. I hid him for three weeks before the cops came. And do you know what? He never gave me a penny. He kept *her* in style, she never wanted for a fiver, but me—*I* had to work. I started taking in boarders and I've got six here now. If you think it's easy—" She paused, angrily, but drowned her anger in another long drink of beer.

"Where did he get his money from?" asked Mannering.

"He's got a fortune tucked away under different names," she answered with great confidence. "Got jewels and *objets d'art* in half-a-dozen places, too. If you ask me, he had about five homes, with a wife in each. Talk about sailors!"

"And he stored some stolen valuables in each, is that it?" Mannering asked with rising excitement.

"That's what I *think*. I know if you go to that blonde's flat in Chelsea it's full of antiques and things. Worth a fortune, if you ask me. I went there once," went on Mrs. Knight with obvious satisfaction. "I nearly tore her eyes out."

"Did he always work alone?" asked Mannering.

"Whenever he could, but there were some jobs he needed help with," said the woman. "Now and again he worked with a chap called Leo. They made a good pair, they did— why, I was hiding Chick Leo up here when the cops were after him, and it was all I could do to keep him out of my bed. That's the kind of friend he was. Bloody lecher. So was Blackie but he didn't pretend he wasn't." That hint of reluctant admiration came again: it was almost nostalgia. "I daresay Blackie would have been a decent sort, but he was sent to a reform school when he was only a lad, and he's been in and out of prison ever since. The only way he could look after himself was to use his fists and his head. I've seen him—" She broke off, and swallowed the rest of her beer.

"You've seen him do what?"

"Break the arms and the legs of a man who sold him out," stated Mrs. Knight, clearly.

"What do you think he would do to you if he knew you were talking to us like this?" demanded Mannering.

She looked at him very straightly. There was silence for what seemed a long time, and then she said:

"I'm not safe while he's out. My children aren't, neither. I want him back inside. I'm not a squealer, I won't give him away to the cops, but when it comes to threatening Mr. Mannering it's a different cup of tea. I don't know who you are," she repeated, making Mannering wonder whether in fact she had a suspicion, "but I know old Josh here's helped a lot of people out plenty of times when things have been tough. So when he came to ask me if I could tell him where Blackie was, I told him: Yes. *And* I know. But it will cost Mannering five hundred quid. I'm not in it for kicks." She turned to Larraby and said challengingly: "You knew that, Josh, didn't you?"

15

HARD FACTS

Almost as soon as the woman finished, on a note of near-defiance as if both hopeful and fearful, Larraby said quietly: "Yes, I knew that." He turned to Mannering, and asked in a curiously flat voice: "Do you think Mr. Mannering would pay five hundred pounds?"

"If he was sure the information was genuine," Mannering said.

"Soon fix that side of it," declared Black Knight's wife. "Don't pay until afterwards. If you give me your word on it, Josh, five hundred quid in cash if I tell you right, then I'll tell you now."

Larraby said very quietly: "I will guarantee the five hundred pounds, Mrs. Knight. And pay you fifty pounds now." He took out his wallet while staring again at Mannering. "Don't you think that's fair?"

"Yes," said Mannering.

Larraby selected five ten-pound notes and placed them on the table by the woman's side. She glanced at them but did not pick them up.

"Ta," she said. "He's at Farnham in Surrey."

Mannering's heart began to beat very fast.

"A house in a street called the Borough," she said. "He's got a floosie tucked away there surrounded by antiques and objects. If you ever let on where you learned this you'll have signed my death warrant. But you know that, don't you, Josh?"

"I know it," Larraby replied. "He'll never find out."

"Do you know the name of the woman?" asked Mannering.

It couldn't be Griselda, he almost prayed. Griselda could not be more than thirty, and so been only twenty when Black Knight was arrested.

"Goodman," answered Mrs. Knight. "Dolly Goodman."

.   .   .

Mannering was still aware of the shock of that news when he left the house with Larraby. They walked to the car quickly, and Mannering took the wheel. As Larraby closed the door a man came out of the shadows between two parked cars: a policeman. When he saw the man's helmet, Mannering almost froze. Larraby's voice did not hold a tremor as he said:

"Good evening."

"One o'clock at night's a funny kind of evening," the policeman replied. "What are you doing out so late, sir?"

"It isn't really late for a night-owl like me," Larraby protested mildly. "We have been talking to Mrs. Knight, about a room for Mr. Marriott here—Mr. Marriott is looking for comfortable board and lodging. He—"

"At this time of night?" the policeman derided.

"Really, what time we visit anyone is entirely our business," Larraby said sharply. "If you have any doubts, go and ask Mrs. Knight."

The policeman said: "Mind if I have a look in the car and the boot?"

"I see no reason why you should, but if you insist I shall not try to stop you. Isn't that how you feel, Mr. Marriott?"

Mannering said in the near Cockney voice:

"I feel mad and I'm getting madder."

The policeman took a cursory look inside the car, and opened the boot. Only the spare wheel and some rope and tools were there.

He moved back and the danger seemed to have past, when a police car turned into the street, and almost immediately, one turned in from the other end. On that instant, alarm flared up in Mannering.

"Sit tight, Josh," he warned.

He switched on the engine, and made it roar. The policeman who had backed away came rushing forward. Mannering did the only thing he could; thrust his arm out of the car, placed his hand on the other's chest and sent him hurtling backwards. As the man staggered the police car behind screeched to a standstill. In seconds, there would be no chance.

In a flurry of understanding, Mannering knew that Knight's wife must have called the police. He rammed the gears into reverse and crashed into the stationary police car. One man, half out, went flying onto the pavement. Mannering slid into bottom gear and drove forward. The second police car was pulling into the kerb, and Mannering swung out and past it.

He gasped: "All right, Josh?"

"Ye-yes," Larraby gasped in turn.

Mannering reached the corner and swung round it. Two cars were near, but not dangerously. He passed them and took two sharp turnings: just ahead, a bus passed; so this was a main road. He pulled in close to the corner. There was no sound of anyone behind them as they climbed out. Almost as soon as they reached the corner a taxi appeared, its *For Hire* sign bright.

When they were inside, Larraby gave instructions to the driver and they sat back, to recover from the fierce burst of activity. When at last he spoke, Mannering said:

"So we can't trust Mrs. Knight."

"I—I am dreadfully sorry, sir. I thought she was wholly reliable. I suppose someone else *could* have told the police a stranger was there," Larraby added tentatively. When Mannering didn't reply, Larraby went on drily: "I do agree, sir. It isn't likely."

"I'll need a fast car," Mannering said, out of the blue.

"You can get one at the garage where we are going, sir."

"Good." Mannering pushed his hair back and went on in a disillusioned voice: "It really is a night for shocks, Josh."

"So I gathered, sir. Is the name Goodman familiar to you?"

"It certainly is," Mannering replied. "It's the name of the antique dealer I called on in Farnham." He paused. "I wonder whether we can trust Mrs. Knight after all. If you were watched by Black Knight, and if he jumped to conclusions about me, then he could have called the police."

"It is just conceivable, sir," Larraby conceded; then he asked with some hesitation: "What will you do, sir?"

"Go to Farnham, of course," Mannering said.

"It will be *very* dangerous."

"Josh," Mannering said. "I can't see that I've any choice. If Black Knight is there I've got to get him. I think he is, more likely than not."

"But—"

"There aren't any buts," Mannering said, a little wearily.

"I think there's one alternative course of action," insisted Larraby. "You could tell the police that you recognised Black Knight running down the stairs at the house in Farnham, and you have reason to believe he's at the house now. They would certainly go and look for him, sir."

"And what if he slipped through their fingers?" asked Mannering, gruffly. "No, Josh. I've got to go back." He gave a ghost of a laugh. "It's the last place they'd expect to find me. With luck I'll find Knight there and then call for the police—and be back in Chelsea before anyone realises that I've been away."

"I hope very much that you're right," said Larraby, unhappily.

Mannering thought: but he doesn't think I am. Larraby was badly worried, of course; as worried as Lorna, and with even more cause. He, Mannering, was more concerned with the possibility that Larraby was wrong about Mrs. Knight. Everything she told them had sounded very convincing, and yet—she *had* talked of her husband with that nostalgic admiration. And it had all fitted in too neatly for coincidence.

The taxi was now bowling along the East End where Larraby had many friends. It stopped outside a garage with a blazing neon sign, reading: 24-Hour SERVICE. Mannering paid the driver, and as he drove off a man came out at once. Larraby, remarkably spritely, went towards him.

"Hallo, Jim," he called.

"Well, what do you know," the other exclaimed. "How're things, Josh?"

"Fine, fine," said Larraby. "My friend wants a nice, reliable fast car for a day or two. What do you have available?"

"How about a 1969 Jag?" suggested the garage hand.

Ten minutes later, Mannering was driving a black Jaguar along the East End Streets, then along the Embankment. When he came in sight of Big Ben, he saw that it was nearly two-fifteen. A surprising amount of traffic was about, and barges moved sluggishly down the river. Now and again he could see the surface of the Thames like polished black glass, reflecting the light on either side of the river and the bridges. It was quiet and peaceful and for a while he was inwardly calm.

Soon, he was driving down Guildford's cobbled streets. A policeman was trying the doors beneath the famous clock. He went on to the Hog's Back, where traffic was speeding. A car flashed by, a police car hurtling after it.

Reaching Farnham, he turned into the Borough, which was lit by only a few lamps. It was utterly still. He switched on his headlights and drove slowly. As he neared Number 47 a policeman showed up, in a doorway. On the other side of the road another man stood in shadow. Beyond the wall which enclosed the house a police car was parked, two men inside it. Now he had no doubt: the police had been warned that there would be a raid.

Who could have warned them but Mrs. Knight?

He went a mile or two along the road to Odiham, then took a side road and turned the car. He didn't drive off at once. Obviously it would be madness to try to get in. Even if Black Knight were there, it would be disastrous. So, what could he do? Already by leaving Chelsea in disguise, he had put himself hopelessly in the wrong. Now he must do so again.

Should he visit Goodman?

He began to drive, slowly, this time with his headlights dimmed. There was an upward flash of light from another car's headlights and he saw the silhouette of a man on the roof. Cooper meant to take no chances at all! The policemen in the car glanced at the Jaguar but did not follow. At the T-junction at the end of the road, he turned left. The headlights shone on the windows of cottages, shops, two pubs, some flowers in a tiny garden, window boxes: and then the hanging sign outside Goodman's shop, saying *Antiques*. Not far along was the car park of a public house, and he turned in, switched off his lights, and waited for a few minutes.

One car passed; then silence fell.

Soon, he got out, closed the car door lightly, without latching it, and walked towards a lane which led to the backs of the houses, but it was difficult to judge which was Goodman's. He went back along the main street. The bottle glass of Goodman's windows would be impossible to break, and it would be too risky to climb up to a first-floor window.

He reached the door, and immediately used his picklock. A few twists, a few turns, and the lock clicked back. Were there chains and bolts? He pushed the door top and bottom, and it yielded, but the middle was still fast; the single bolt, then, was there. He had a tool which could slide the bolt back if there were a space between door and frame to get a grip. On this old wood it would be possible to cut an inch or two away, but that would take time.

The tool he had was like a pair of calipers, which would grip the bolt. There was a fraction of an inch gap. He took out a small chisel and pared away perhaps an eighth of an inch; the wood was soft, probably wormy. He tried the caliper tool again, and there was room.

The headlights of a car showed in the distance.

There was a shop doorway near enough for him to hide in, and he waited for the car to pass; then another and another. He peered in both directions but there was no sign of a policeman on beat duty. He went back to the door, gripped the bolt, and edged it backwards, a tiny movement each time.

Then, the grip slipped; he had reached the end of the bolt.

He pushed, and the door opened. Another car passed as he was stepping inside, but it didn't slacken speed. He closed the door behind him, and leaned against it, breathing hard with tension. At last he was satisfied that he hadn't been heard. He switched on a pencil-thin torch. The door on the left, leading to the shop where he had bought the lion, was locked, but none of the other downstairs room doors were even closed. A storeroom, cloakroom, dining-room, kitchen and a scullery; in the light of the torch all looked old-fashioned. He went back to the passage and the stairs, reached a narrow landing, and then saw a very pale light in a room over the shop.

This door was open.

He could hear even breathing as he listened at the door. A glow from the street added to the night light, and he saw two small beds and a cot. So this was a children's room!

Goodman was a widower—

Mannering turned to the next room, and found the door ajar. He pushed it wider. After a few moments he could pick out the shape of different pieces of furniture, and the shape of a bed—a double bed, with one occupant, a woman with blonde hair which showed up very plainly.

Dolly Goodman? The 'blonde bitch'?

He drew back, closing the door very quietly.

There were only two doors left, and one led to a bathroom where the W.C. cistern gurgled. The other, then, was Goodman's room. This door was closed but not locked. Mannering opened it. Someone sighed, just behind the door. In his sleep? There was no other sound and Mannering pushed the door open wider. He switched on the torch but kept the beam away from the bed which stood behind the door. The room was small, and crowded with furniture. It was little more than a box-room, and much smaller than either of the others.

The breathing was heavy and even; almost snoring.

He lowered his torch and the beam fell on the top of Goodman's head.

Now Mannering began to search the room. It was a long time since he had done this with someone sleeping so near him, all unaware, but gradually the old feeling of confidence and normality returned. He opened drawer after drawer, cupboard after cupboard but did not find what he was looking for: the rest of the Ottenshaw jewels.

He found nothing of value anywhere, even when he tried everything except the cabinet by the side of Goodman's bed, and the bed itself.

Goodman slept on, heaving breathing rhythmic and on the same tonal level.

Mannering pulled open the door of the cabinet and found nothing; in the drawer were oddments that a man would carry about with him: wallet, loose change, keys, a comb, a penknife. He sifted through all these and then turned to the bed. There was a chance, a slim one, that the jewels were under the pillow. There was a greater chance that if he had them at all they were in a safe or some hard to find hiding place.

Very gingerly, he pushed his hand under the mattress, but he could not get far enough. Then, he moved his hand under the pillow—and immediately Goodman stirred. Mannering stayed still. There was a marked pause in the other's breathing, and when it was resumed the sound was different. He felt sure that Goodman was feigning sleep now, and if the man behaved in character he would make a heave upwards. Slowly, as if furtively, Mannering withdrew his hand; and then made a circle with the thumb and forefinger of his left hand, and half-circled Goodman's throat. The man heaved upwards, violently, but Mannering's pressure was such that all he did was choke himself. His feet and arms thrashed but he could not free himself and he began to gasp. Mannering maintained his hold but shifted his position and sat on the bed, trapping Goodman's legs.

Gradually, he eased the pressure.

"Can you hear me?" he demanded in his assumed voice.

"*Lemme go!*" gasped Goodman.

"Can you hear me?"

"I'll break your neck!"

Mannering pressed harder and the spluttering protests

were cut off. After a warning pause, he said in a harsher voice:

"Can you hear me?"

"Yeah—yeah, I can hear."

"I want the jewels you took from Griselda Leo's flat," Mannering said.

"Je-je-*jewels!*"

"The diamonds and emeralds. Where are they?"

"I haven't got them," Goodman said hoarsely. "You want a man named Mannering, not me. What the hell made you think I took them?"

Mannering took a wild shot in the dark.

"I thought your sister Dolly wanted them for Blackie Knight," he said.

The other man went absolutely still. He seemed almost to stop breathing. His eyes had a baleful look in the dim light, but when he spoke his voice was hoarse as if with fear.

"How did you know about Blackie and Dolly?" he demanded hoarsely. "How did you know?"

16

DOLLY

There seemed to be terror in Goodman's manner; and Mannering could feel his nerves twitching and jumping. Mannering eased the pressure but Goodman made no attempt to spring at him. That question had shocked him far more than anything about the jewels.

Mannering said: "I have a lot of friends."

"He—he'll kill her," Goodman gasped. "He'll kill her."

Mannering drew back from the bed, groped for and found the light switch. The light shone out, very bright, from above the head of the bed. Goodman covered his eyes with his hand. Mannering moved to the window and drew the curtains. Goodman's hair was tousled, he looked ashen grey. There was a tear in his blue and white striped pyjamas at the first button. His collar bone showed up vividly and there appeared to be a dark cavity on each side, beneath them.

"What makes you think Black Knight would kill anyone?" Mannering asked.

Now, Goodman was staring at him as if in hopes of recognition. His lips were unsteady and his words ran into one another.

"He'd kill anyone who crossed him. He—he'd kill Dolly like a light!"

"Give me one reason why," urged Mannering.

"She was his mistress before he went to prison. She—she got married, she and her husband were going to emigrate but—but—but he died. She was frightened Knight would find out, and went back to her maiden name. Oh God, he'll kill her."

It was pointless to argue.

It was shattering to know that Goodman felt so sure how Black Knight would behave. Mannering recalled the man at Quinns: he recalled the way his wife had talked about him. One thing was absolutely certain: Black Knight struck fear into anyone who had crossed him.

"Where is Dolly?" Mannering asked.

"She—she—why should I tell you?" Goodman found some spirit at last.

"It looks as if you're going to need a lot of help," Mannering said. "Or Dolly is. Is she the woman in the next room?"

"Yes, yes, she—"

"How long have she and the kids lived here?"

"Since he was released," Goodman answered. "She—she knew the first thing he'd do would be to come after her. He—he's the devil himself."

"Now, come," protested Mannering. "He wouldn't expect a woman to wait that long for him while he was in jail."

"You—you don't know him. He once—" Goodman ran a trembling hand across his face. "He slashed the face of one girl who didn't wait for him, he—I tell you he's the devil himself!"

"Does he know your sister married?"

"No," Goodman said. "That is she didn't tell him, but he'd be sure to find out."

"Where was she living before she came here?"

"In London. She—she just panicked, packed the kids up and came here. I had to take them in, but if he ever finds out where they are, God knows what he'd do to me as well as Dolly."

From the door, a woman said in a husky voice: "He'd

cut your throat." The door opened and a woman came in
She wore a dressing-gown wrapped tightly over a nightdress
with frills at the neck and throat. Her flaxen, braided
hair was in a net, she had no make-up but only the traces
of night cream; there was a striking quality of beauty in
her face, and the folds of the dressing-gown hinted at an
hour-glass figure. Her eyes were fine and bold, the fair lashes
sweeping upwards in fine curves. She looked at Mannering
and asked: "Who are you?"

Mannering said: "I don't like Black Knight, either."

"I didn't think they'd let him out for another two years,"
she said, heavily. "If I could get out of the country I'd go
tomorrow, but I've got no money and my only capital is my
face and my kids. Oh, God," she said, and sat down heavily
on the side of the bed. "If you won't tell us who you are,
you can tell us what you want."

"He—he thought I had the jewellery," Goodman muttered. "That bloody Mannering—" He broke off.

"If I had the jewels I'd flog them so fast you wouldn't
be able to see London Airport for dust," Dolly Goodman
said, still wearily. She looked at Mannering from half-closed
eyes. "You see before you a combination of Don Quixote
and George Washington. The original honest man—my
brother Frank. He could have made a fortune but he preferred to be honest and poor. A hell of a lot of good it's
done him." She talked as if Goodman were not there.
"When I think—" She broke off, and let her hands flop
in her lap. "So what's the use. He's got a clear conscience
and Blackie's on his back. I've got the muddiest conscience
in London and I've got Blackie on my back, too."

"Dolly, for God's sake shut up," her brother muttered.

"Okay. I'll shut up. Only I can't stand these long, heroic,
long-suffering silences of yours. I'd rather you slapped my
face and told me I was a whore and I'd made my own
bed and I could lie on it. Or is it *lay* on it? I never

could tell those two words apart. But let me tell you I know what they mean. You wouldn't believe it but Blackie was the first man who ever laid me. I was born before the great Age of Permissiveness. And when he went inside I thought I could be true. He really was my Black Knight. It wasn't until afterwards, when I discovered how many women he'd ruined, how many faces he'd slashed—"

"*Shut* up!" her brother cried.

"Okay. I'll shut up. Only I can't stand the suspense. Where do you come into this, mister? Who told you my brother had those sparklers?"

"He was there about the time they disappeared," Mannering said.

"Who told you?"

"Mannering's manager," Mannering said.

"Mannering!"

"Mannering is in trouble," Mannering volunteered, and added in a tone of deep satisfaction: "That won't do him any harm, the big know-all. Old Josh Larraby came to me for help. He said he wanted someone to prove the missing jewels were still here. If they were, that would let Mannering out. I've got quite a reputation for breaking and entering—you don't need telling how justified that is."

"No," Dolly said. "He's good, isn't he, Frank?"

Goodman was staring at Mannering, who went on with a husky laugh: "If I could have laid my hands on those jewels, Mannering would have had to pay through the nose. I look after Number One all the time."

"Did Larraby pay you to come here?" demanded Goodman.

"Only a bit on account—"

"You make me sick," Goodman rasped.

"Now, Frank—"

"Well, he does. The whole rotten stinking mob make me sick. Larraby pays him good money to do a job for Mannering and all he can think of is how to squeeze more out of them. You make me *sick*." He glared at Mannering.

"Don't pay any attention to him," Dolly urged. "Honesty is a disease with him. Let me tell you something. He could have made a fortune selling stuff for Blackie and Leo. They had it stored away all over the South of England. He had only to sell it piece by piece and he would have made a fortune. But oh, no. It was stolen, he wouldn't soil his lily-white hands."

Mannering was reminded of Mrs. Knight, for in Dolly Goodman there was a blend of affection and scorn, admiration and condemnation. She did not understand her brother and did not share his thinking but she liked him, more because of his attitudes than anything else.

"Oh, put a sock in it," Goodman said to his sister, but something of the bite had gone out of his voice. "If Mannering hired someone to come and look for the jewels here, he couldn't have taken them, could he?"

"Never heard of a cross double-cross?" asked Dolly.

"He wouldn't have gone to all this trouble if he already had them," Goodman said impatiently. "So if he doesn't have them and I haven't, who took them?"

"Mannering would give a fortune to find out," Mannering said.

He was aware that people were outside; several men, he suspected. Who would they be but the police? He did not want these two to know but there was a risk that everything they said was being overheard.

"I daresay Mannering *would* give a fortune. And if Mannering didn't take them, then maybe he didn't kill the old man," went on Goodman. "He may have been telling the truth all the time."

"Frank—" began Dolly.

"*Be quiet!*" Goodman was staring at Mannering with great intensity, and his body had gone very rigid. His sister subsided. "The jewels were there when Mannering heard the doors banging—Griselda told me that. And they'd gone when he left for the second time. So someone must have come up and stolen them while Griselda was in her uncle's room. She went in there and saw him and fainted. She doesn't know how long she was out. It must have been then when those jewels were stolen, so who could have taken them?"

"Just tell me, and I'll go and check," said Mannering.

Goodman looked at him in disgust.

"And sell them to the highest bidder—you wouldn't help Mannering to clear himself. Well—" His tone lightened and his face brightened. "That's one good thing, Mannering seems to be innocent. It was a hell of a shock to find that a man with his reputation was a crook." He relaxed, sitting back on his pillows and actually smiling.

"That helps me a fat lot," said Dolly, sarcastically. "Mannering's a saint and a hero just like you. I'll die happier because of that." Quite suddenly she buried her face in her hands, sobbed in a heartrending way, and spoke in a voice so thick that the words were hardly audible. "What am I going to *do*? Oh God, what am I going to *do*?"

Goodman, startled, leaned forward, then scrambled forward clumsily and put his arm round her shoulders. He did not speak but looked imploringly at Mannering, as if asking: Can't you help? Can't you?

After a few moments, Mannering said: "There's one thing you could do."

"What's that?" asked Goodman, hoarsely.

"Help to put Black Knight back in prison."

"But what's he *done*?" cried Goodman.

Mannering said: "He's had these stolen goods hidden away."

"But he's served his sentence for stealing them."

"He'd earn another if he started to sell them," Mannering said.

"Good God! No!"

Mannering moved to the window and stood with his back
to it. One of the children cried out and Dolly raised her
head sharply, but there was no other cry and she dropped
her hands onto her lap. Her cheeks were tear-stained.

"The only thing I know," she said, "is he'll find me. I
might just as well have stayed at home, he'll find me
sooner or later. It's the kids I worry about most. What the
hell are they going to do if anything happens to me?"

Mannering thought: *she is absolutely convinced that
Black Knight will kill or seriously injure her. She takes it
for granted.* This introduced a new element into the affair
which was already complex enough. He stared at the
woman's hopeless face, and seemed to see another, even
more despairing: Griselda's. Here were two women in
terrible fear.

Was Griselda's fear of Black Knight, too?

He said: "You could ask for police protection."

"That would make him madder," Dolly said. "But if we
could put him away—" There was a spark of hope in her
voice. "If I could have just a year or two longer I could
make enough money to get abroad. God, how I hate living
here! I'm frightened all the time. Even when my husband
was alive, when—when we were in bed, I'd think of Blackie,
and I'd be useless, absolutely useless. If—"

"Goodman," Mannering said, "do you know if Griselda
Leo knows Black Knight? Or knew him before he went
inside?"

Goodman echoed almost stupidly: "Griselda?"

"Your innocent little sweetie," Dolly sneered, but her
brother ignored her.

"*Griselda!*" exclaimed Goodman, and suddenly he looked
appalled. "Do you mean—" He broke off, his mouth wide
open. "Great Scott! If he—if he stored some of the loot

there, if everything at Number 47 was stolen, if he went back to see it and found she'd sold a lot of it—my *God*!"

Dolly was now sitting upright, and her eyes seemed huge.

"Where did she get the furniture and the antiques from?" asked Mannering.

"Her—her father."

"Do you know who her father was?"

"No," Goodman answered, almost choking. "He came here with his wife and Griselda not—not long after Black Knight went inside. And Blackie had a partner, *Leo*." He scrambled off the bed and began to pace the room, looking like a scarecrow, bony knees sticking out of torn pyjama legs, one elbow sticking through his sleeve. "Dolly, *think*. You told me they were partners, you wanted me to sell their stuff for them."

Dolly said: "Blackie went inside but Leo wasn't involved in the job the police and Mannering caught him for, so he was in the clear, though they'd both been stacking away stuff for years."

Goodman turned excitedly to Mannering.

"Just before Blackie was caught he asked me to handle the things he'd stolen. He'd got antiques in a warehouse and *objets d'art* and jewellery all over the place. He—he offered me fifty per cent of everything I got for selling it —didn't he, Dolly?"

"I nearly went down on my knees to ask you to do it," Dolly said. "But you were Honest Frankie, it was all you could do not to tell the police about the offer."

"The point is, he had to do something with it," said Goodman, hoarsely.

"And if Leo did look after it all for him—"

"In the Borough—"

"And then sold half of it—"

"And Blackie discovered where he was—"

"That could bring Black Knight down here," Mannering

said, much more calmly than the others.

"He'd blame Griselda!" cried Goodman.

"To hell with Griselda—" began Dolly.

Goodman spun round on her: "Don't talk like that about her! She's had a hell of a life, nothing's gone right for her, and now she's had a shock she might never recover from. Don't talk about her like that! Do you hear?"

Dolly looked at him in swift and sudden contrition.

"I'm sorry, dear," she said. "The trouble is, I feel sorrier for myself than for anyone else. If I could only think of some way of getting out from under it would be better, but—"

The child in the front room cried out again.

"That's Ronnie," she said. "Having one of his nightmares. As if there weren't enough nightmares in this family already!" She looked at her brother, and stretched out a hand. "Don't hate me for this," she said. "Try not to, anyway. But you could have been fooled by Griselda, you know. She could have been selling stuff off and piling up a fortune for herself. *No!* Don't jump down my throat, Frank, it *is* possible."

And Mannering said: "It's possible that the jewels weren't stolen, too. She might have hidden them in the flat. I hadn't time to make a thorough search."

"If you think that's possible why the hell don't you go and search now?" cried Goodman. "You broke in here easily enough, why don't you break in there?"

17

THE CHALLENGE

Goodman was so tense that his hands were quivering and his voice shook. And Dolly started, as if agreeing with her brother about this, if nothing else. Mannering could almost 'see' the policemen, but the temptation to try to get in, in spite of them, was overwhelming.

He said: "The place is swarming with policemen."

"So you're not very good," sneered Goodman.

"Don't be daft, Frank," Dolly said. "If there are a lot of police there no one could break in. But it *is* possible."

"That Griselda's a liar and a cheat, you mean. Griselda—"

"How long has she been frightened?" asked Mannering.

"Frightened?" Goodman stalled. "Why?"

"*Years*," interjected Dolly.

"How the devil do you know that?" Goodman demanded, furiously.

"Because you've been telling me about her for years," Dolly retorted. "You said she seemed to change after her father died." That squared with what Griselda had told him, Mannering reflected, in a curiously distant part of his mind. "But if she'd been selling stuff—"

"Be yourself!" interrupted Goodman. "She lives in that attic, has to rent off all the rest of the place to keep the house. If she were selling Black Knight's stuff she'd live like a queen. *I* trust her absolutely."

"I trusted Blackie once," countered Dolly. "That was when I was in love, too." When Goodman made no retort, she went on bitterly: "And just imagine, I came away from London to get away from Blackie, and what do I do? I run straight into him."

"You never said a truer word," Black Knight said, and he thrust open the door and came in.

.   .   .   .   .

He stood, enormous and imposing, in the doorway. The light, so bright, showed the sallow skin at his cheeks and nose and forehead. His mouth closed like a trap, and he stared only at Dolly. All her fears and all his menace showed. Mannering felt as if he were watching two people play out their lives, while knowing that his was inextricably involved.

The child cried out again.

Dolly reared back against the wall, positively cringing.

"If you think you can hurt Dolly—" Goodman began, and he took a long step forward. "I—"

Black Knight swept his left arm round, and gave him a tremendous buffet on the side of the face. Goodman went flying, struck the wall opposite the bed, and leaned against it, crouching. His breathing was very hard.

"Come here," Black Knight said to Dolly.

"Blackie—"

"Don't Blackie me, you bitch. Come here."

She was also crouching back against the wall. Her bare feet stuck out beneath the dressing-gown, giving her a curiously helpless look. Both she and the big man behaved as if Mannering wasn't here but every now and again Mannering saw Blackie give a quick glance out of the corner of his eyes.

"Blackie," Dolly said hoarsely, "I've got three kids."

"I told you to come here," Black Knight growled.

The unbelievable, the awful thing, was that very slowly

Dolly began to obey. It was as if his glare was hypnotic and compulsive and the woman was drawn to obey against her will. She hitched herself forward, and as she did so, Black Knight spun round, right fist clenched, and drove a blow at Mannering's face. It was powerful enough to send him flying, perhaps to break his nose. But Mannering, alert every split second, moved his head enough for the bunched fist to flash past, then brought his own clenched fist down onto Black Knight's biceps. The man gasped, taken completely by surprise. His arm fell by his side. Mannering gripped his other wrist and twisted, then thrust the thick arm upwards, behind his back. Black Knight let out a stream of obscenities, and back-heeled. He caught Mannering's shin a glancing blow but did not free himself.

Dolly was leaning against the wall, astounded.

Goodman began to move, gulping. staring as if he could not believe his eyes.

"Now we can have a little talk with you, Blackie," Mannering said, and when the other's great body tensed he pushed upwards and said harshly: "If you try that again I'll break your arm."

"My God, when I get you I'll break every bone in your body," Knight growled.

"Who told you Dolly was here?" Mannering demanded.

"To hell with you!"

"Who told you? Your wife?"

Black Knight said: "If you think I'm going to talk—"

"I think you're going to talk and talk fast," Mannering said. "Did your wife tell you?"

"She—hell, yes."

"Did she tell you about Larraby and me visiting her?"

"She told me the lot, you bloody fool," growled Knight. "If you think she would let me down, you're mad."

"I think you could terrify her into doing whatever you wanted," Mannering said. "Did Leo take over your loot before you went inside?"

"Supposing he did, the double-crossing little swine."

Mannering jerked his arm.

"Did he?"

"Yes! My God, when I get free from you—"

"Your only hope of getting free from me is to tell me the truth," Mannering said grimly. He felt a great sense of triumph but was keyed up to an almost unbearable point of tension. "Why did you kill Griselda's Uncle Ted?"

"I didn't kill anybody!"

"I saw you at the house."

"You didn't see me kill anyone."

"Why did you kill him?"

"You witless fool," growled Black Knight. "I wouldn't spend the rest of my life in prison for killing that spineless pig. I went to fix Mannering."

"You killed Ted so as to have Mannering framed," said Mannering, roughly.

"You don't get anything right," said Black Knight. "I didn't kill him. I went to talk to him."

"What did you want to know?"

"Where his precious niece had stowed the money and the rest of my stuff."

"Did he tell you?"

"He said he didn't know anything about it, the liar. I left him alive."

"I don't believe you."

"I left him alive," Black Knight insisted. "I saw Mannering there and went and fixed his car. My God, I—"

He broke off.

Somewhere nearby a car roared, and almost at the same instant, footsteps sounded at the back. A car door slammed. Next moment there was a heavy knocking on the street door. On that instant of utter stillness, Black Knight back-heeled and pulled hard; and this time Mannering let him go.

The child cried out and went on crying.

Mannering, hardly daring to breathe, realised that there was no way of escape this time. He wouldn't have a chance —unless perhaps there *was* a faint chance of escaping in the confusion caused by Black Knight's bull-like rush for safety. He glanced at the window. It was just wide enough to climb through, but if the police had effectively surrounded the place, someone would be outside.

Downstairs, there was a crash of sound, as of a door banged back against the wall. A man bellowed:

"Stop there! Stop!"

Mannering swung out of the room as Dolly darted along the passage towards the front room and the crying child. Another child began to cry on a shrill note, Dolly's voice sounded, with the calm of desperation: "There, there, darling, it's all right, Mummy's here."

But the children went on crying.

Mannering reached the passage which led to the top of the stairs. At the top, looking downward, stood Black Knight. He was huge and menacing as he filled the head of the stairs—physically frightening and capable of doing great damage to anyone in his way.

Halfway up the stairs was Chief Inspector Cooper; Cooper himself.

"Give it up, Knight," Cooper said. "You haven't a chance and you know it."

As he spoke, Black Knight drew his hand from his pocket, and thrust a gun towards the policeman. There was a glitter in his eyes and his lips seemed red-wet against his black beard and very white teeth. Cooper drew in a sharp breath.

"Put that away," he ordered, and took a step upwards.

At that moment of time, Mannering saw the slight tensing in Black Knight's hand, the lack of compassion in his eyes, and he knew that Cooper realised he was very close to death. It was as if both of them were struck with stillness for that split second. In it, Mannering could have got away, back through the child's bedroom, up on to the roof to safety.

The thought did not enter his mind.

Using every ounce of strength he launched himself over the railing and Black Knight was taken completely off his guard at the sight of a man hurtling towards him. He squeezed the trigger, but he was off balance and the bullet smacked harmlessly into the wall. As Mannering's feet swung by him, he staggered back, dropping the gun. Mannering, gripping the wooden rail, twisted round so that he could land on the stairs between Black Knight and Cooper. As he did so, Frank Goodman came rushing along the passage, striking at Black Knight who was pressing against the wall.

Mannering felt Cooper's hands grip him at the waist. Somehow, he steadied, one foot on one tread, one on that below, with Cooper leaned against the wall to steady him, Goodman beating Knight about the head and shoulders, gone berserk, the children crying, Dolly's voice pitched on an even higher note of desperation.

"It's all right, I tell you. It's all right!"

Cooper said to Mannering: "Are you all right?"

"I—" began Mannering, and then had a moment of sheer panic, for he was about to speak in his natural voice, which would have betrayed him to Cooper. He gulped, and muttered: "I'm fine," in his assumed voice. Slowly descending, he pressed against the banisters to make room for two of Cooper's men.

A young uniformed policeman said: "I hand it to you for guts."

Mannering forced a smile.

"Do you have a drink?"

"I've got a flask," another policeman volunteered from the front door.

Soon, Mannering was sitting on the corner of the table in the kitchen, warmed by a tot of whisky. He was alone. The police had pulled Goodman off Black Knight, and the children's crying had stopped. All the police were crowded into the little house, and Mannering could have walked straight out. But that twisted leap had pulled his back muscles; he already felt sore. And he wasn't yet sure that he would be wise to go even if he could. Cooper owed him a great debt. He might be able to help this 'stranger'.

Suddenly there was another commotion, a roar of sound, gasping, thudding and thumping. Mannering looked up the staircase and saw Knight, handcuffed to the biggest policeman, and struggling with uncontrolled fury. Just above him stood Cooper.

Cooper simply chopped the side of his right hand onto the back of Black Knight's neck, and the giant gasped and collapsed, almost toppling the man to whom he was handcuffed. Cooper grabbed his shoulder, and between them they got him down the stairs and along the hall passage. A police car pulled up, outside; so it would have been useless to have run. One man opened the rear door, Knight was half-dragged and half-pushed in, still handcuffed to the big officer. The door slammed. A plainclothes man took the wheel and the car moved off.

Cooper turned towards Mannering.

He was dishevelled, his collar was torn and his tie hanging loose, and there was a swelling on his left cheekbone. But he still looked a formidable man in complete control of himself. Mannering wondered what was passing through his mind; whether he fully realised that he had been so close to death.

He said: "I've got a lot to thank you for."

"Forget it," Mannering said.

"Not for a long, long time," said Cooper. "He meant to kill me."

"Yes, he's a killer. And you've got him."

"He might have killed me and he might have killed some of my men,' said Cooper in a flat voice. He stared at Mannering as if puzzled. It was just possible that he saw something familiar, that something had gone wrong with the disguise, so that he could see through it. "Why did you take the risk?" he asked. There was only intense curiosity in the question. "You took a hell of a chance."

Mannering said: "Did you think what the odds were when you came towards him?"

"That's different. It was my job."

"I wanted him caught, too," Mannering said.

"Why?"

"Because he would make life hell for a lot of people, including Goodman's sister—the woman upstairs."

"Pure altruism?" Cooper's face was set in scepticism.

"Not only that."

"What else?" insisted Cooper.

Mannering knew that his answer had to be convincing; knew that Cooper was a difficult man indeed to fool. Half-a-dozen answers flashed through his mind, only to be rejected out of hand. He was taking his time, perhaps being too long. There were movements up and down the stairs but none in the room above, where the children were.

"*What else?*" repeated Cooper, as if his patience was running out.

Mannering drew a deep breath.

"All right," he said. "I'll have to tell you. I work for John Mannering. I mean, I do sometimes. Black Knight was at the house in the Borough this afternoon. Mannering thinks he murdered the old man there, and planted half the jewels in his car. And he threatened to kill Mannering this afternoon. Mannering's under a kind of house

arrest, he can't do anything to help himself, so he hired me
to come and talk to Goodman, who's a friend of the Leo
girl. And he wanted me to look for the four pieces of
jewellery—the missing pieces." Mannering paused, and
moistened his lips. Cooper was peering at him so intently
that it was hard to be sure that he didn't see through the
disguise. "When I got here I discovered that Goodman's
sister had been Knight's mistress, and because she married
after he was jailed and didn't wait for him, he was going
to disfigure her. Anyhow, when he came, taking us by surprise, that's what he threatened to do. That's an evil man,
Inspector. He would have killed you, he would have gone
on killing and disfiguring and torturing for as long as he
lived. I had a chance to stop him. Saving your life was
incidental to all the rest." He shifted his position, and
shrugged. "That's the truth and all there is to it."

There was no way of telling whether he had been convincing, and he was sure only of one thing: he could do
nothing more now.

Cooper did not nod or speak but continued to look at him
with piercing intensity; and any moment Mannering expected him to call him by his true name.

18

HELP?

As they stared at each other, footsteps sounded in the passage, and a man appeared in the doorway.

The man hesitated until Cooper turned from Mannering, and said:

"What is it?"

"Do you want to talk to Mr. Goodman, sir?"

"Has he made a statement?"

"Yes, sir."

"Did he say anything about this man?"

"Not very much, sir, except that he claimed to work for Mannering, and thought he—that's Goodman, sir—might have some of the jewels stolen from Griselda Leo's place this afternoon."

Mannering thought: that will help.

"Did the woman talk?" asked Cooper.

"She was Knight's girl friend before he went inside. He seems to think once a woman's his, she's his for keeps. She thought he was going to kill her, and she thinks she would have been killed if this man hadn't stopped him."

"*Twice* a hero," Cooper said. It was almost a sneer.

"Any man who can get the better of Knight twice in half-an-hour or so is all right by me—sir," the other added, hastily. Something in his manner suggested that he thought Cooper was bearing down heavily on the stranger, and he wanted to ease the pressure.

"And by me," Cooper agreed drily. "I'll read Goodman's

statement and question him later if I have to. And Mrs.—what's her name?"

"She's known here as Mrs. Goodman."

"What's in a name?" Cooper asked tolerantly. "Have the house watched back and front, we don't want any more trouble. Are the children all right?"

"Their mother got them off to sleep again, sir."

"So they should all have a quiet night," remarked Cooper. He was obviously doing a practised best to be affable. "I'll be along in a few moments."

"Very good, sir."

The man went off, apparently satisfied that his mission had been successful. Mannering, who felt that the pressure had been eased a great deal, felt it coming back slowly, remorselessly. There was something very unpredictable about Cooper, and although there was now supporting evidence for his, Mannering's, statement, there was no way of being sure that the other was convinced. Cooper straightened his tie at last, and then asked:

"What's your name?"

"Turner—Guy Turner."

"How did Mannering get in touch with you?"

"His man Larraby knew where to find me."

"And where did he find you?" demanded Cooper.

There was a hint that he was needling Mannering now: that the policeman was rising above the man, and duty was forcing gratitude into the background.

"At my digs," Mannering said.

"Where?"

"Number 14, Harcourt Road, Whitechapel," Mannering answered.

That was in fact the home of Larraby's son and daughter-in-law, and the accommodation address he always used with the *alias* Turner. If the police did check it would be confirmed that he had a room there; nothing could be proved against him.

The promptness of the reply seemed to satisfy Cooper for a moment; and then he asked with whip-like speed:

"How do you earn your living?"

Mannering shifted his position further back on the table. Outwardly he was calm, inwardly his heart was thumping. The pressure of the questions was remorseless. If he were once caught out in a lie he would be taken to the police station and questioned with ruthless thoroughness. A vague answer wouldn't do; but how could he be specific?

There was one possible way.

"I'm a runner for antique dealers and picture dealers. I get by." A runner was a well-known character in the trade; a kind of lookout man who had a fair knowledge of works of art of all kinds, and carried information about them to the trade.

"What do you do on the side?" asked Cooper.

Mannering said flippantly: "I break-and-enter, deal in stolen jewels—that kind of thing. Is that what you want to hear?" He slid off the table, his voice changing to one of sharp challenge: "Do you want to question me at the station? Are you taking me in?"

"Why should I take you in?" asked Cooper, evenly.

"That's a good question," Mannering said. "I've another: why are you keeping me here?"

"Where will you go if I let you go?"

"I shall go to Number 14, Harcourt Road, Whitechapel," Mannering replied tartly. "It's not much more than an hour's drive at this time of night."

"Why don't you stay here?" asked Cooper. "Knight will come up before the local bench in the morning and you may be needed to give evidence. Would you have any objection?"

"You mean, evidence against Black Knight for shooting at you?"

"Attempting to cause grievous bodily harm," Cooper corrected.

"It would be a pleasure, but where would I stay?"

"I've a spare room," Cooper said, evenly. "Why, my wife will be very glad to cook breakfast for a man who saved me from being shot." He smiled and put a hand on Mannering's shoulder. "Have you any objection?"

"No," answered Mannering. "I'd be damned glad. I'm just about all in."

"I'll drive you," Cooper said. "I'll have to go round to the station afterwards but there's no need for you to."

Mannering said warmly: "Thanks. Thanks very much."

It was strange, sitting next to this powerful man with the curiously hard manner, to pull up outside a thatched cottage on the outskirts of the town, a cottage where a lamp was burning in the thatched porch. It was strange to be taken in the back way, given coffee and biscuits, then taken upstairs.

"Be as quiet as you can," Cooper pleaded. "The youngsters will give us hell if they wake up."

"How many?"

"A boy and a girl. Twins."

"Lucky man," said Mannering.

He followed Cooper across a creaky landing and along a narrow passage. At every step he had to duck huge beams, passing others supporting the white walls. Suddenly, Cooper turned into a room. It had a sloping ceiling which ended in a wall little more than two feet high.

"This is two cottages knocked into one," Cooper said. "The bathroom's next door. Sleep as long as you can—I won't disturb you unless there's an emergency."

"You're very kind," Mannering said, as if embarrassed.

"You've a short memory," said Cooper. "Good night."

He went off, making hardly a sound, and soon, the purr of his car engine told Mannering he had driven away.

Mannering sat on the wooden arm of an old rocking chair and looked at the chintz-covered bed, the chintz curtains, the simple charm. Then he began to undress.

What was Cooper really up to, he wondered.

Had the detective the faintest idea that he was Mannering? He was a difficult man to read, and Mannering judged he was the kind who would sacrifice anyone, friend, wife, relative, if he thought that his job demanded it.

What was he up to?

Had he recognised Mannering for what he was?

Every nerve in Mannering's body seemed to relax as he stretched out in bed, wearing only his vest and pants. His calf muscles twitched and his shoulder and neck muscles ached, but slowly awareness of pain faded.

It was a funny thing...

Sleeping in a policeman's house...

It had been a narrow shave with Black Knight.

Well, the man was in custody now. Odd that he, Mannering, should have brought about his downfall twice in succession. God, he was tired! But tiredness was easing out of his arms and legs, his neck and body. It was very quiet here. Quiet and comfortable. Warm. He was sinking off to sleep. Incredible thing—in a policeman's home, the policeman who was the cause of his bid for safety. Irony! Crazy—irony. He was tired. Gosh! How tired—

He dropped off.

* * *

About that time Lorna, asleep after a restless hour, heard a ringing sound. It didn't stop, and at last she opened her eyes. It was still dark. There was a bang on the door, then more ringing; and a man called out:

"Open, in the name of the law."

She pushed the bedclothes back and switched on the bedside light. As she struggled into her dressing-gown she felt a flood of fear that the police would find out that John had gone. She put on the hall light, and the ringing stopped. She tied the sash of her gown, then opened the door.

Gordon of the Yard, with two other men, confronted her.

"Sorry to disturb you," Gordon said, obviously finding it hard to conceal his delight. "I want Mr. Mannering to come along with me for questioning."

Lorna made herself say: "He—he's not here. When I woke, his bed was empty. He—"

Gordon said: "My God, he's fooled us!" He waved a slip of paper, obviously a search warrant, and stalked past Lorna, his men following. For two or three minutes the police moved steadily about the flat, looking under beds and into cupboards. Then Gordon let down the loft ladder and went up to the studio. When he came down he was as pale with anger as Lorna was pale with anxiety.

"You'd better get dressed and come with us," he growled. "We'll want to ask you some questions. And the sooner you tell us where your husband is, the better for you. He's wanted on a charge of murder."

* * * *

Mannering did not hear Cooper come home, and in fact did not hear anything for a long time. When at last he was aware of sounds, they seemed a long way off; and they were familiar and unfamiliar. Children's voices. Then a woman said: *"Hush!"* Immediately the voices were subdued, so low that they could not have woken him. Had they, when louder? It was daylight. The chintz curtains were unlined, and he could see the brightness of the sun. *What time was it?* He looked at his wristwatch on the bedside table, squinted, and at last read: 11.20. Good Lord! He pushed the bedclothes back and climbed out of bed. His disguise was more than a bit smudged, and he did what he could to repair it, then saw a large dressing-gown over a chair. He hadn't noticed it before. He put it on, opened the door—and started back, for he was face to face with an attractive woman wearing slacks and a white shirt. She had dark hair which fell almost to her shoulders.

"Why, hallo!" Mannering said weakly.

And then he realised that he had used his normal voice.

Would that one slip betray him? he wondered desperately.

It would have done with Cooper, but would it with her?

She had a startled but laughing look, obviously taken by surprise as much as he.

"Good morning! I was coming to see if you were awake."

"Well, I'm glad to prove it," Mannering said in his assumed voice. "But it's so late."

"My husband says you didn't get to sleep until well after four o'clock."

"But it's after eleven now!"

"The hearing is at twelve-thirty," she told him. "And a car will be here to pick you up at twenty past twelve. So you've plenty of time. Would you like some tea before you bath?"

"It would be wonderful!" Mannering enthused.

"I'll bring it up in five minutes," promised Mrs. Cooper. She moved easily as she ducked beneath a beam at the head of the stairs. When she came up again it was with a pleasing little white morning tea set. She placed it down by the side of his bed as he sat on the edge, and then looked down at him. She had wide, blue-grey eyes, now dimmed with tears.

"I just—I just must say thank you," she said in a low-pitched voice. "Hal told me what you did. I just must *say* thank you. Thank God for you!" She stretched her hands out for a moment, then drew back and hurried out of the room. In a hoarse voice she called: "Breakfast in half-an-hour."

She closed the door.

Breakfast was of bacon, eggs and sausages, toast and coffee, served in a bright chintz-curtained modern kitchen. The morning newspapers carried a brief story of the murder of Edward Leo, and the fact that Mannering had been involved in a car accident near the scene of the murder. Completely oblivious of what had happened at Chelsea, he ate with relish. The children were playing in a sandpit in the garden. Mrs. Cooper was moving about the house, now and again the vacuum cleaner groaned. The car arrived five minutes after Mannering had finished eating. He called out that he was going, and Mrs. Cooper came hurrying down to see him off.

"Mr. Mannering," she said. "I really mean it. I will *never* be able to thank you. And nor will Hal."

Mr. Mannering, she had said.

There was not the slightest doubt. The one thing that saved him from showing his consternation was his make-up: his cheeks showed neither colour nor pallor.

"You've been very kind," he responded in his assumed voice. "I'm glad I was able to save your husband's life." He held her gaze for a few seconds, then turned and got into the police car, beside the driver. If he was really known as Mannering, wouldn't there be two men in the car? He waved to her. She held up one hand in a farewell salute as the police driver started off along a narrow, paved road with a large Georgian house standing back, its lawns and flowerbeds immaculate, followed by a row of thatched cottages. When the car turned into a main road, Mrs. Cooper was still there.

The driver said: "Good morning, sir. Do you mind if I say something?"

"Say what you like," invited Mannering, but was very, very wary.

"That was a bloody fine thing you did last night. Everybody's talking about it. It would have been hell if anything had happened to old Hal—to Mr. Cooper. Most respected and most liked man in the Force. If anything had happened to him—well, it didn't." The driver sniffed: it was as if he were fighting an emotional outburst. "Very popular man in Farnham as well, sir. Not so long ago he dived into the river over near Guildford and pulled out a couple of kids who would have drowned. Made him a proper hero. So—anyway, thank you, sir."

Mannering made vague noises.

The car turned into a main street and then towards the new police station. As they drew up, Mannering was aware not of one or two but of dozens of people waiting on the steps, including policemen. Then he realised that he was facing a battery of cameras. As he touched the door a policeman came forward and opened it. There was an outburst of applause, in which the police joined. Others came hurrying out of the police station, and also joined in. Cameras clicked, bulbs flashed, a television camera whirred. Mannering's heart was pounding. As Mannering he had known such receptions but never as Turner. Would the disguise resist the probing eye of the camera? These photographs would be splashed all over the London evening papers as well as local newspapers, and millions would see them; including almost everyone who knew him as John Mannering.

19

UPROAR

As this realisation struck Mannering with an icy chill, he saw Cooper walk out of the main doors of police head-quarters. There was another ripple of applause which grew in volume as the people made a path for him. He stretched his hand out to Mannering and the cameras clicked and whirred and flashed again. Then Cooper put up both hands.

"That's all—we're going into court. If Mr. Turner wishes he can make a statement to the Press afterwards." But his wife knew Mannering *as* Mannering. He motioned Mannering back into the car and soon they were being driven off, the driver sitting very square at the wheel. "I told them they could have their pictures if they would ask no questions," Cooper said. "Not one did—the Press are good sorts if you give them a fair deal. Did my wife look after you well?"

"Extremely well," Mannering said warmly.

"Good," applauded Cooper, and went on almost without a pause: "Unless Knight has a defending counsel down from London and wants a hearing, we shall offer evidence of arrest and ask for an eight-day remand. You'll only be needed if he asks for a hearing."

Mannering said: "I see."

The court-house was new and modern, in a concourse of concrete buildings with attractively arched windows and doorways. The courtroom itself was in light oak panelling, and but for the clock, witness box, magistrate's clerk's table and the press gallery, looked almost like a theatre. There was ample room for both the public and the magistrates themselves.

As Cooper led Mannering forward, there was a clatter of movement, and suddenly the Press swarmed into the press gallery. Soon the public came in, behind Mannering, to a rumble of footsteps and muted voices. A policeman called: "Quiet, please, quiet." The magistrate came next, and the usher—a policeman with very white hair—called "Silence!" Two men, one elderly, the other middle-aged, approached the bench, and a very small woman followed them. The elderly man was the chairman of the magistrates. Now there was a kind of hum of expectancy, before the chairman said in a tired-sounding voice:

"Will you have the accused sent in."

"Send in the accused," called the magistrate.

". . . the accused," echoed the usher.

From a staircase well on one side, quite close to Mannering and Cooper, a big policeman appeared, his left arm stretched behind him. Immediately, Black Knight appeared, arms stretched in front of him. They were handcuffed together. A second policeman, as big as the first, came close behind and Black Knight was also handcuffed to him. Black Knight himself looked like an enormous captive bear.

There were the formalities. The name of Wilfrid Arthur Knight was established, the chairman enquired about the charge, a policeman who had been at Goodman's house last night took the stand, then the oath.

In an expressionless voice he recited the fact that Knight had been found on enclosed premises, that he had been in unlawful possession of a gun, and that he had savagely attacked with that gun a police officer.

"Is the accused represented?" asked the chairman, and the middle-aged magistrate and the woman nodded, as if this were of great consequence.

"No, sir," the magistrate's clerk reported.

"I don't want anyone to represent me. I represent myself," rasped Black Knight. "If the bloody police had done their job properly yesterday I wouldn't be here now. Instead of coming after me because I was after the bitch of a woman who betrayed me, they ought to have caught Ted Leo's murderer. They know who it is all right, they just don't want to charge him, that's all." He glared at the magistrates, who seemed dumstruck, and at the clerk, rising in protest. He dropped back into his seat. "One law for the rich and one for the poor, that's what's the matter with this bloody country." Suddenly he switched his fierce gaze on Cooper, and thrust his head forward aggressively. "Why didn't you arrest Mannering, that's what I want to know. And why didn't you charge that sonofabitch sitting beside you. He had no more light in Goodman's house than I had. Bloody coppers—why don't you do your job instead of picking on the likes of me?"

Mannering sat absolutely rigid.

The chairman said in his tired voice: "I really cannot see the relevance of the accused's remarks."

"Your worships," said the police officer in the box, "the prisoner has been extremely violent while in custody and we have reason to fear he might cause grievous bodily harm to others if he should be set free. We ask, therefore, for a remand in custody while enquiries are being made. As for his remarks about the murder here in Farnham yesterday, a warrant has been issued for the arrest of a Mr. John Mannering in that connection and the police in London and elsewhere are assisting us in locating the said John Mannering."

He stopped.

Everyone in the court now turned towards the magistrates, while Mannering sat next to Cooper, feeling as if he had been turned to ice.

. . . .

The woman and the middle-aged magistrates leaned towards the chairman, and there was a whispering behind hands with which they shielded their faces. Then the chairman emerged as the others swayed back into obscurity.

"The accused is remanded in custody for eight days," declared the chairman.

Suddenly, there was an upheaval in the dock, as Black Knight made a gargantuan effort to pull himself free, dragging his massive captors in front of him. Other police rushed to help restrain him. For a few moments there was uproar in the court. Cameras clicked and flashed against all laws. At last, Black Knight was overpowered and dragged away, at last the police and the ushers restored order: and all this time Mannering sat without moving.

Then Cooper said: "All right, Mr. Turner. You are free to go."

Mannering heard him. At first, the words made no sense, but suddenly they did, and he realised that he was acting strangely and that Cooper was staring at him. He stood up.

"Thanks," he ejaculated. "Well—you shouldn't need much more evidence against Knight. What's this about Mr. Mannering?"

Cooper's eyes seemed to be the most piercing Mannering had ever seen.

"A warrant was issued during the night," Cooper said, and added with great precision: "There wasn't any choice. There was a great deal of *prima facie* evidence even before the dead man's niece said she saw Mannering attacking her uncle. She came round from her sedation quite rationally, and made the statement of her own free will. She stated that Mannering had given her a cheque for five thousand pounds as payment for her silence. We found a cheque in her flat. I can tell you another thing," Cooper went on, as they moved along the centre gangway of the now nearly empty courtroom. "Scotland Yard officers went to arrest him at his Chelsea home last night and he had vanished. He's on the run. That's pretty clear indication of guilt, isn't it?"

"Yes," Mannering said as briskly as he could, "but not necessarily his own. Didn't Mannering tell Larraby that Knight was the killer?"

"There's no evidence Knight was in Farnham yesterday afternoon," Cooper said, in a tone of cold finality.

They went into the foyer and then outside. More cameras faced them and now reporters hurled questions, mainly at Cooper. Mannering stayed for a few minutes, then slipped away unobtrusively. Soon he was in a side street, where few people were about. As Turner he was a free man, but as Mannering he was on the run and the hunt would be remorseless. As he saw it now his one hope was to find proof that Black Knight had been in Farnham at the time of the murder.

Certainly Cooper held no brief for the man who had been remanded, but—how could he ignore Black Knight's accusation.

Was he satisfied? Was the Press? Or was he simply waiting for the right moment to pounce?

Mannering reached a main street, and recognised it as a road leading to the Borough and towards the inn where he had left the hired car. He walked mechanically, thinking ceaselessly.

Why had Griselda lied?

He had believed in her, trusted her absolutely, become involved in this affair for her sake, so—why had she lied?

He had helped her. She had talked with such eager enthusiasm about him being an honest man. He had actually given her that cheque, and it could be the key piece of evidence to condemn him.

Why had she lied?

He reached the Borough and looked along it, past some fruit stalls. On one corner were a mass of parked cars near the lovely houses. He could just see Number 47. He went on. Goodman's shop had a 'closed' sign in the window: that was hardly surprising. Mannering went past and reached the inn where he had left his car.

It had gone.

In a strange way, this blow seemed the worst of all. His car, Turner's car, had gone: his one means of transport, of getting away from Farnham without a fuss. He felt as if he had been struck a physical blow as he stood there, gazing at some small modern cars and small old cars, at every kind of car but his. He was still reeling when a woman crossed the road and reached him. At first he didn't recognise her, she was so well made-up and nicely dressed. As she smiled, he knew that it was Dolly Goodman. He did not want to see her. He did not want to see anyone who was involved in the case yet. He would come out of this mood soon, he would have to begin working as Turner, to find out the truth, but now he felt sick at the very thought.

Dolly's smile faded.

"You don't look so good," she said, touching his arm. "Mr. Turner, Frank and me want to thank you any way we can, God knows what would have happened but for you last night. And Frank moved your car, it's parked behind the shop. Come over and have a word with him, won't you?"

He crossed the road, heart lifting because of the car, yet very wary. How had they known it was his? How had Goodman got the ignition key? He felt in his pocket, and touched his keys, and the question reached almost screaming point.

Then Dolly pushed open the door and stood aside for

him to pass. He went in and saw Bristow coming along the passage from the kitchen.

.   .   .   .   .

Bristow wasn't smiling, but he put out his hand. Beyond him was Goodman, behind Mannering, the woman. A dozen thoughts flashed through Mannering's mind, including an almost word for word recollection of what Bristow had said on the telephone last night.

Bristow's voice was very loud and almost aggressive.

"Good morning, Mr. Turner," he said.

Mannering's return grip was very strong.

"I must say you're the last man I expected to see," he said. "What's brought you, Superintendent?"

"Plain 'mister' now," Bristow reminded him. "As I've told Mr. Goodman, I've come down in the hope that you or someone down here can help Mr. Mannering. You've heard about the warrant for his arrest, I suppose."

"It was announced in court," Mannering said drily. "And I gather that Griselda Leo says she saw him attack old Ted Leo. That pretty well finishes Mannering, doesn't it? If you get fingerprints, opportunity, motive *and* an eye-witness he's in a spot no one can help him out of, Super— Mr. Bristow. And I don't know that I want to stick my neck out, trying."

"So you've got feet of clay after all," Dolly said in a tone of disgust. Mannering had never found it so difficult to act a part; never thought he could be affected by scorn in the voice of a woman like Dolly.

Before anyone could retort or comment, a child called from upstairs, an eager: "Mummy, Mummy!" Dolly Goodman went up, without glancing at Mannering, and soon she was at the very spot where he had fought Black Knight.

Mannering glanced up at her, sourly.

"What does she expect? That I'd stick my neck out by habit?" He was bursting to find out what Bristow wanted, but Goodman was still in the kitchen, and within earshot. Slowly, Mannering began to take notice of him. At first it was because he wanted the man to go away but the motive changed. Goodman looked ashen-faced and sullen, presumably because of what Griselda had told the police.

Bristow went on as if he were not there.

"I don't know how much you know but I can tell you this: if we can find the rest of those jewels and prove that Mannering didn't take them, there will be a break in the evidence against him. But the strongest evidence is Griselda Leo's statement."

"That she saw him attack her uncle?" Mannering asked, feeling sick at heart.

"Yes."

"She's a liar," Mannering said.

"She must be," agreed Bristow. "Mannering wouldn't have killed Leo, even if he'd had a motive. It's utterly unbelievable. So the girl lied, or—"

Mannering saw Goodman stiffen with sharp interest.

"Or, she thought it was Mannering but in fact it was someone else," Mannering said, to quieten him. "What do you want me to do? I don't promise I'll do it, though. I'm not promising anything."

"I want you to search Griselda Leo's flat," Bristow told him. "The police have had a go but I want you to—"

Goodman stepped forward.

"You leave Griselda alone," he said hoarsely. "She's had enough trouble as it is. You stay away from her place, do you hear?" His fists were clenched, he looked ready to take them both on.

Bristow spun round on him, angrily.

"So you love her and you trust her. Well, we know Mannering and we trust him. Someone's lying and it has to be

Griselda Leo. If you'd any guts you'd go and make her tell the truth."

"She's a damned sight more honest than you ever will be," shrilled Goodman. In spite of his beard, he looked very young. "You keep away from her."

"Oh, let's get out of here," Bristow growled. "I could do with a sandwich, they do them at the pub across the road." He pushed past Mannering and opened the door as if utterly disgusted. Mannering followed him out. They waited for several cars to pass, and then crossed the road.

"John," Bristow said, "you are in a hell of a spot. Lorna was at the Yard half the night."

"My God! If Gordon—" Mannering began.

"Calm down, calm down," Bristow urged. "She's back home. She said you both went to bed and just before the police arrived she woke up and found you had gone. They had to check her story. They had Larraby at the Yard, too, and all the assistants have been questioned at Quinns. Gordon even questioned me!" There was an edge to Bristow's laugh as they turned into the pub. "The key evidence is Griselda Leo's, of course. I doubt if she'll change her tune—"

"Have you seen her?"

"I spent half-an-hour with her when she returned home this morning," Bristow answered. "She's lying in her teeth." He entered the saloon bar of the inn, and immediately turned to a window overlooking the main road. "I'll get the drinks," he said. "You watch the shop."

He came back in a few minutes, with two glasses of beer and some pork pies, as Mannering belatedly remembered the snacks Lorna had put in his pockets. He took a beer, said: "No thanks" to the pies, and then saw Goodman come out of his shop. Goodman looked up and down before hurrying towards the Borough and turning into it.

"He's gone to warn Griselda," Mannering told Bristow. "I

know what I'd like to do, Bill. Go and search the shop in case he's holding the missing jewels for her."

"Why do you think I goaded him to leave?" asked Bristow, smugly. "The woman won't object. She thinks he's making a fool of himself over Griselda." He ate the two pies quickly, finished his beer, and added: "Let's go."

When they reached the antique shop, the door was open. A child was laughing upstairs, but no one was in sight. Mannering and Bristow went into the shop itself, and began the search for the missing jewels. Whoever had removed them from Griselda's room and planted half of them in Mannering's car, would, of necessity, have hidden the other half: to find them would therefore establish the thief. All the time Mannering was aware of increasing fear; whenever he thought of Lorna being questioned he felt a surge of rage, but that wouldn't help.

He opened drawer after drawer in the old pieces, opened every box, looked in every vase; and so did Bristow. They examined the dusty wooden floor, but found no trace of a hiding place and no sign of the jewels. Bristow finished, wiping his forehead.

"Where next?" he asked.

"Goodman's bedroom," said Mannering.

They ransacked the bedroom, and as they did so, Dolly Goodman passed along the passage, carrying one child and shepherding the others down the stairs. Soon, the front door closed. Mannering and Bristow searched the other bedrooms and the bathroom; finally the kitchen and two other rooms downstairs, and found nothing.

"They could be anywhere," Bristow said, despairingly. "If we could only make the Leo girl change her story you'd be in the clear." But there was hopelessness in his voice.

"Bill," Mannering said, when they were downstairs in the shop again.

"Yes?"

"This is all part of a pattern. Even being allowed to search here—Dolly made it very easy; suspiciously easy. Knight's wife was pretty glib, too. Into my parlour, said the spiders. It's all been too easy from the beginning. Everybody hates Black Knight and everybody pushed me a little nearer to a trial and conviction for murder. Before we know where we are the police will arrive here and we'll both be charged—"

The words were hardly out of his mouth before a police car drew up outside the shop.

20

'INTO MY PARLOUR'

There were two policemen in the car. They sat for a few moments before one opened the driver's door. Mannering was already on the move towards the kitchen, and Bristow followed. Mannering pushed open the kitchen door. Beyond was a paved yard opening onto a service road, and the hired Jaguar was parked at one side. No one else was in sight; no policemen and no neighbours. Mannering sped towards the car and was at the wheel and starting the engine before Bristow got in beside him. There was a banging sound as Bristow slammed the car door.

"They're banging at the front," he said. "I wonder if you're right to run."

"I'm right," said Mannering. "She told you she'd leave the place clear for us, then went out and telephoned the police." He edged the car out into the alley and turned towards the Borough, into which the service lane ran. There was only just room. He reached the Borough, and pulled into a parking place.

Dolly Goodman was pushing a pram, with her youngest lying down and a two-year-old sitting up at one end; the oldest child, perhaps five years old, was holding onto the handle of the pram. Mannering waited until she was within a few yards, and then got out. Bristow emerged on the other side. Dolly looked up and saw them—and her mouth dropped open. Mannering reached her side in a couple of strides.

"All right, Dolly," he said. "Where are the jewels?"

"Je-jewels?" she stammered. "I don't know what—"

Mannering suddenly lifted the child out of the pram, held her at one shoulder and rummaged under the smelly mattress. He felt a package and drew it out. A dozen passers-by watched, but none so breathlessly as Bristow. Dolly opened her mouth wide, as if to scream. Mannering lifted the package and held it high. At the same moment he called clearly:

"How many of you saw me take this package out of the pram?" He looked interrogatively at a passing youth who answered almost eagerly:

"I did."

"Why you bloody little liar!" Dolly screeched.

"But I *did* see him!"

"So did I," another youth called.

"He certainly took it out of the pram, there was nothing in his hands when I came up," an elderly man in a khaki-coloured linen jacket called.

"Thank you, sir," Mannering boomed. "Would you be good enough to open the package?"

He leaned across and thrust it into the man's hands, while Dolly now stood speechless. Mannering placed the child back, and it stayed quite happily. The elderly man began to unwrap the package, and had it almost open when a police car drew up. Two men got out and came forward, but as they neared the elderly man the sunlight shone on something very bright which sent out scintillas of vivid light.

"My goodness!" the elderly man exclaimed. "These are diamonds. And—and—what *are* these green jewels? Diamonds and—and—"

"Emeralds!" someone nearby called out.

"Diamonds and emeralds!" gasped the man holding the package.

The policemen stepped forward. Dolly Goodman suddenly spun round on Mannering and kicked viciously at his groin, but he dodged to one side. Then she began to rage at him, her profanities screeching through the warm summer air. One of the policemen took the jewels, which were wrapped in cotton wool, while the other rasped at Dolly:

"Shut up! You're frightening the wits out of those kids."

The children *were* whimpering.

Mannering touched the policeman on the shoulder, and recognised the one who had been on the steps of the police station that morning. He saw the softening of the man's expression.

"Yes, sir?"

"I want to go and see Miss Leo," Mannering said. "Will you tell Chief Inspector Cooper that I'll come and tell him about this find in half-an-hour or so?"

"If you'll just tell me what happened, sir."

"*Filthy, stinking liar!*" Dolly began again.

"I found them in this woman's pram," Mannering told the man. "You might check the crowd for witnesses. You'll find dozens." He turned and walked off, with Bristow at his side, and the police made no attempt at all to stop him. They were at Number 47 in less than a minute, and hurried round to 47d.

The door was open; the lock which Mannering had forced hadn't yet been repaired. He pushed the door wider. As if to square his conscience Bristow called: "Is anyone at home?" in a muted tone. No one answered. Mannering went upstairs first, and found the living-room door open. He could see many of the treasures round the walls, and he could hear deep breathing. As he reached the doorway, he heard Frank Goodman saying in a husky voice:

"But why—why would you lie? Why would you send an innocent man to prison?"

The girl didn't answer.

"Just tell me—*why?*" Goodman demanded helplessly "It's wicked, it—"

Griselda Leo gasped: "They made me!"

"Who—who do you mean?" Goodman asked, his voice still hoarse.

"*They* did."

"Blackie? But Blackie's in custody, he can't frighten you now."

"But she can," Griselda gasped.

"*Who is she?*" Goodman's voice rose to a scream.

"Your bloody sister!" cried Griselda. "Oh God, it's been awful, awful. Black Knight left these things with my father —and his women kept coming and making me sell some of them. They threatened to tell the truth about my father if I didn't, so—so I kept selling pieces. one after the other. When it wasn't Dolly it was Norah—"

"Who—who is Norah?" Goodman broke in hoarsely.

"Blackie's wife, who do you think? She hated Blackie, so did Dolly, but they're evil. Evil! While he was in prison they kept blackmailing me. When they wanted the jewels it was the last straw. I couldn't bear to part with them, it was too much. That's why I sent for Mannering. I thought he'd help me. I didn't know Blackie was coming out of prison so soon." She broke off, sobbing. "I just didn't know."

Mannering was tempted to move forward but Bristow restrained him, his hand on his arm.

"But why did you say you *saw* Mannering kill your uncle?" Goodman asked helplessly.

"Oh, you'll never understand!" she cried. "They *made* me. I've been selling stolen goods most of my life, and they knew it. They swore they'd give me away if I didn't name Mannering. And—and—and I would have come under suspicion, too. Of the murder, don't you understand? I didn't have any choice, I just had to do what they told me."

Goodman said in a strained voice: "Even though it

meant condemning an innocent man."

"But he meant nothing to me! And they don't hang mur-
derers any more." She broke off, and her voice changed,
there was a rustle of movement before she gasped imploringly: "Frank, you wouldn't let me down, would you? You
say you love me, now *prove* it. Don't tell the police, I
couldn't stand it. I hate prison, I—I hate it. My father
used to tell me it was like being buried alive. *Frank!* You
won't tell the police!"

"But I haven't any choice," Goodman said in a hopeless
voice. "I can't let an innocent man suffer for—*Griselda!*"
He screamed the name. "Griselda!"

Mannering thrust open the door. Griselda was standing
over Goodman who was reeling back against the sofa table,
hands stretched out to fend her off. In her right hand was a
knife, the blade very bright. When she saw Mannering she
flung the knife at him but it missed by inches and buried
itself into the wall.

.   .   .   .   .

It was early evening.

Mannering and Bristow left the Bush Hotel in the Jaguar
and drove round to the police station. No one took any
notice of them. They knew that Cooper had charged both
Dolly and Griselda, who were being held; and also knew
that Cooper had since talked to Black Knight, telling him
what the police now knew. Ten minutes earlier, Cooper had
telephoned and asked them to come round.

By the time they left Cooper, Mannering knew, Lorna
would be here; she was driving down for him and Bristow
would drive the Jaguar back. Mannering, still disguised,
had talked to her from a call-box; even now he could recall
the relief in her voice.

"Oh, John," she said. "I was so afraid."

Soon, they pulled up outside the police station, a constable opened the door, and they hurried up the now-deserted steps. They were shown at once to the office where Cooper had first interviewed Mannering. Cooper looked a little tired about the eyes, but his voice was brisk and his composure still very apparent.

"Well, it's virtually all over," he told them. "What I have to say is all off the record, of course."

"Of course," echoed Mannering.

"Every word," promised Bristow.

"Thank you, gentlemen. You know the basis of it, no doubt: that years ago the two thieves Knight and Leo, worked together, that after Mr. Mannering found the evidence which sent Knight down for a ten-year stretch, Leo took care of everything they had stored away. While Leo was alive all went well, but when Griselda 'inherited', Knight's wife and his mistress, working together, blackmailed her to get what they considered their rightful share. All clear until then?"

"Yes," Mannering said, slowly; and he could picture it all.

"They didn't expect Knight out of prison so soon, and he didn't let them know that he had earned maximum remission," went on Cooper. "He'd heard from rumours in prison that all wasn't well. When he got out, his wife and ex-mistress got together again. They had to find a scapegoat, and it had to be someone Knight would believe was guilty. So they chose John Mannering. They told Knight he had been forcing Griselda to sell, that they hadn't been able to help themselves. There was just one man who knew the truth, however—Ted Leo, who sponged on Griselda all the time. They had to kill him to make sure he couldn't talk to Black Knight."

Mannering caught his breath, so vivid was his understanding.

"But how did they get here?" Bristow demanded.

"Very early," Cooper replied. "They rented one of the flats—47c, The Borough. The floor beneath Griselda, that is. All they had to do was nip from their flat to the staircase, go up and kill Ted Leo, and sneak back into the flat. They timed it perfectly. Black Knight went up and found Ted with his head battered in. They placed the doorstop on the stairs—meaning to fix Black Knight. Your coming when you did was an embarrassment which they soon turned to advantage. Knight was blundering about, poor dupe, and Mannering was a handy victim, too. You had Knight wanting to fix Mannering, and the women fixing Knight to make sure we caught him before he could do them any harm. Are you following?" Cooper demanded abruptly.

"You'll never know how closely," Mannering said.

"There isn't much more," said Cooper. "Everything worked according to both their long-term and emergency plans, but Griselda remained a problem. She was genuinely shocked. In fact, quite terrified. What she wanted was enough money to run away with, just to turn her back on the past. That was the idea behind the cheque Mannering gave her. Simple security. We found the cheque but not a letter which we've since found, in reverse, on the back of a sheet of carbon paper."

"So Mannering is free from suspicion completely," Bristow said with great relief.

"I wouldn't say that," objected Cooper, and the others went very still. For the first time Cooper reminded Mannering of the way he had been the previous night; as if he had something up his sleeve and was waiting to use it.

"Why not?" demanded Bristow.

"We have Griselda Leo's admission," said Cooper. "But we haven't yet discovered why Mannering ran away last night, or where he went to. A man was seen leaving Knight's house. He knocked out two policemen and damaged a police car. There is reason to suspect that it was Mannering."

"If that's the most you've got on him, why not forget it?" Bristow argued.

"Little things can lead to big ones. If the Yard can hold Mannering on that charge who knows what else we'll find on him?"

Mannering looked at him narrowly, acutely conscious of his disguise and of Mrs. Cooper's use of his real name. He drew a deep breath before saying:

"If you ask me, it's pretty vindictive."

Cooper stopped, and looked very hard at Mannering, *alias* Turner, and demanded:

"Do *you* know where Mannering was last night, Mr. Turner? You seem very attached to him."

"I do not," said Mannering, his heart thumping. "But I've a deep regard for him."

"I—" began Bristow.

"I have good reason to believe that he was here in Farnham, disguised," stated Cooper. "I have good reason to believe that he forced entry into Goodman's shop. That he—"

"Oh, nonsense!" exclaimed Bristow. "He couldn't possibly have been near Farnham—not after he went back to London, at all events. He was worried out of his wits and came to see me, in the hope that with my knowledge of police attitudes and thinking, I could help him. Whatever idea you have in your head you can forget, Cooper. Mannering can't possibly have been in two places at once."

Cooper's mouth opened. His eyes rounded. And then he burst out into a tremendous gust of laughter.

.   .   .   .   .

"Hal," said his wife. "were you right?"

"What about?" asked Cooper vaguely, as he read the *Evening News*.

"Mr. Turner being Mannering, of course."

"Oh, that!" Cooper put his paper down, and there was merriment in his eyes. "Sweetheart, I can't be sure. I would have put a hundred pounds on it last night, but when a man like ex-Superintendent Bristow says that Mannering was with him and so couldn't be in Farnham, what is a poor country cop to do?"

"Oh," said his wife, and looked greatly relieved. "I—er—I was afraid I'd given the game away."

"What particular game?" inquired Cooper.

"Quite by accident, I called him Mannering this morning," she said. "He didn't seem to notice, but—"

Cooper leaned across from his armchair and gripped her knee with his powerful fingers.

"Some accident," he remarked. "You and Bristow would make a fine pair!"

.   .   .   .   .

Lorna Mannering sat on a pouffe in the study of the Chelsea flat, leaned her head back against Mannering's knees, so that each had an upside-down view of the other. A movement from Swan Lake came softly from a record player built into an oak settle which was three hundred years old. He had finished telling her all he could of the story, and now sniffed the bouquet of brandy in a large bowl-shaped glass.

"And you doubted which side Bristow would be on," she said.

"Doubting Thomas that I was. But never again, darling, never again."

After a pause, Lorna said: "What do you think will happen to Griselda?"

"Nothing much," said Mannering. "They'll let her out on bail, I think. Her defence could be that she was always sub-

ject to blackmail and was not wilfully criminal," Mannering answered. "I have a feeling that when it's all over, she
and Frank Goodman will get married."

A week later, he passed Goodman's shop. But he did not
go in, for glancing through the window he saw Griselda.
She was obviously making order out of chaos.

HELP FROM THE BARON

John Creasey

She was probably a pretty girl. She lay on her back rolling very gently with the swirling currents.

On the night of her twenty-first birthday Francesca Lisle was fished out of the river. A beautiful diamond gave a clue to her attackers. The priceless Fiora jewels had been her father's birthday present. But no-one knew how or where Mr Lisle had acquired them.

It was then that a savage death turned the case into murder. Fortunately the Baron was on the trail of his friends' attackers . . .

CORONET BOOKS

SPORT FOR THE BARON

John Creasey

Why should an Australian sheep-farmer (even a millionaire one) want the Alba insignia?

Nathaniel Brutus, creased grey suit, pink shirt and all, didn't look remotely like a wealthy collector. But once the Baron was convinced of the millionaire's genuine wish to buy the Alba insignia, he agreed to bid for him. Why then did the Baron find himself refusing to up the bid by a hundred thousand pounds at the crucial moment? Why did he infuriate Brutus and risk his own professional reputation?

CORONET BOOKS